The Shadow of a Man by E. W. Hornung

Ernest William Hornung was born in Middlesbrough England on 7th June 1866, the third son and youngest of eight children.

Although spending most of his life in England and France he spent two years in Australia from 1884 and that experience was to colour and influence much of his written works.

His most famous character A. J. Raffles, 'the gentleman thief', was published first in Cassell's Magazine during 1898 and was to make him famous across the world as the new century dawned. It is on this character that this volume is based. Hornung was also wrote a stage play about Raffles as was a gifted poet.

Spending time with the troops he published Notes of a Camp-Follower on the Western Front during 1919, a detailed account of his time there. This was especially close to his heart as his son and only child only child was killed at the Second Battle of Ypres on 6 July 1915.

Ernest William Hornung died in Saint-Jean-de-Luz, in the south of France on 22 March 1921.

Index of Contents

CHAPTER I

THE BELLE OF TOORAK

"And you're quite sure the place doesn't choke you off?"

"The place? Why, I'd marry you for it alone. It's just sweet!"

Of course it was nothing of the kind. There was the usual galaxy of log huts; the biggest and best of them, the one with the verandah in which the pair were sitting, was far from meriting the name of house which courtesy extended to it. These huts had the inevitable roofs of galvanised iron; these roofs duly expanded in the heat, and made the little tin thunder that dwellers beneath them grow weary of hearing, the warm world over. There were a few pine-trees between the buildings, and the white palings of a well among the pines, and in the upper spaces a broken but persistent horizon of salt-bush plains burning into the blinding blue. In the Riverina you cannot escape these features: you may have more pine-trees and less salt-bush; you may even get blue-bush and cotton-bush, and an occasional mallee forest; but the plains will recur, and the pines will mitigate the plains, and the dazzle and the scent of them shall haunt you evermore, with that sound of the hot complaining roofs, and the taste of tea from a pannikin and water from a water-bag. These rude refinements were delights still in store for Moya Bethune, who saw the bush as yet from a comfortable chair upon a cool verandah, and could sing its praises with a clear conscience. Indeed, a real enthusiasm glistened in her eyes. And the eyes of Moya happened to be her chief perfection. But for once Rigden was not looking into them, and his own were fixed in thought.

"There's the charm of novelty," he said. "That I can understand."

"If you knew how I revel in it—after Melbourne!"

"Yes, two days after!" said he. "But what about weeks, and months, and years? Years of this verandah and those few pines!"

"We could cover in part of the verandah with trellis-work and creepers. They would grow like wildfire in this heat, and I'm sure the owners wouldn't mind."

"I should have to ask them. I should like to grow them inside as well, to hide the papers."

"There are such things as pictures."

"They would make the furniture look worse."

"And there's such a thing as cretonne; and I'm promised a piano; and there isn't so much of their furniture as to leave no room for a few of our very own things. Besides, there's lots more they couldn't possibly object to. Curtains. Mantel-borders. I'm getting ideas. You won't know the place when I've had it in hand a week. Shall you mind?"

He did not hear the question.

"I don't know it as it is," he said; and indeed for Rigden it was transformation enough to see Moya Bethune there in the delicious flesh, her snowy frock glimmering coolly in the hot verandah, her fine eyes shining through the dust of it like the gems they were.

His face said as much in the better language which needs no words.

"Then what's depressing you?" asked Moya brightly.

"I dread the life for you."

"But why?"

"I've been so utterly bored by it myself."

Her hand slid into his.

"Then you never will be again," she whispered, with a touching confidence.

"No, not on my own account; of course not," said Rigden. "If only—"

And he sighed.

"If only what?"

For he had stopped short.

"If only you don't think better of all this—and of me!"

The girl withdrew her hand, and for a moment regarded Rigden critically, as he leant forward in his chair and she leant back in hers. She did not care for apologetic love-making, and she had met with more kinds than one in her day. Rigden had not apologised when he proposed to her the very week they met (last Cup-week), and, what was more to his credit, had refused to apologise to her rather formidable family for so doing. Whereupon they were engaged, and all her world wondered. No more Government House—no more parties and picnics—but "one long picnic instead," as her brother Theodore had once remarked before Moya, with that brutal frankness which lent a certain piquancy to the family life of the Bethunes. And the mere thought of her brother accounted for so much in her mind, that Moya was leaning forward again in a moment, and her firm little hand was back in its place.

"I believe it's Theodore!" she cried suspiciously.

"I—I don't understand," he said, telling the untruth badly.

"You do! He's been saying something. But you mustn't mind what Theodore says; he's not to be taken seriously. Oh, how I wish I could have come up alone!" cried Moya, with fine inconsistency, in the same breath. "But next time," she whispered, "I will!"

"Not quite alone," he answered. And his tone was satisfactory at last. And the least little wisp of a cloud between them seemed dispersed and melted for ever and a day.

For Moya was quite in love for the first time in her life, though more than once before she had been within measurable distance of that enviable state. This enabled her to appreciate her present peace of mind by comparing it with former feelings of a less convincing character. And at last there was no doubt about the matter. She had fallen a happy victim to the law of contrasts. Society favourite and city belle, satiated with the attractions of the town, and deadly sick of the same sort of young man, she had struck her flag to one who might have swum into her ken from another planet; for the real bush is as far from Toorak and Hawthorn, and The Block in Collins Street, as it is from Hyde Park Corner.

It may be that Moya saw both bush and bushman in the same rosy light. To the impartial eye Rigden was merely the brick-red, blue-eyed type of Anglo-Saxon: a transparent character, clean of body and mind, modest but independent, easy-going in most things, immovable in others. But he had been immovable about Moya, whose family at its worst had failed to frighten or to drive him back one inch. She could have loved him for that alone; as it was it settled her; for Moya was of age, and the family had forthwith to make the best of her betrothal.

This they had done with a better grace than might have been expected, for the Bethunes had fine blood in them, though some of its virtue had been strained out of this particular branch. Moya none the less continued to realise the disadvantages of belonging to a large family when one wishes to form a family of two. And this reflection inspired her next remark of any possible interest to the world.

"Do you know, dear, I'm quite glad you haven't got any people?"

Rigden smiled a little strangely.

"You know what I mean!" she cried.

"I know," he said. And the smile became his own.

"Of course I was thinking of my own people," explained Moya. "They can't see beyond Toorak—unless there's something going on at Government House. And I'm so tired of it all—wouldn't settle there now if they paid me. So we're out of touch. Of course I would have loved any one belonging to you; but they mightn't have thought so much of me."

If she was fishing it was an unsuccessful cast. Rigden had grown too grave to make pretty speeches even to his betrothed.

"I wish you had known my mother," was all he said.

"So do I, dear, and your father too."

"Ah! I never knew him myself."

"Tell me about them," she coaxed, holding his sunburnt hand in one of hers, and stroking it with the other. She was not very inquisitive on the subject herself. But she happened to have heard much of it at home, and it was disagreeable not to be in a position to satisfy the curiosity of others. She was scarcely put in that position now.

"They came out in the early days," said Rigden, "both of the colony and of their own married life. Yet already these were numbered, and I was born an orphan. But my dear mother lived to make a man of me: she was the proudest and the poorest little woman in the colony; and in point of fact (if this matters to you) she was not badly connected at home."

Moya said that it didn't matter to her one bit; and was unaware of any insincerity in the denial.

"I don't tell you what her name was," continued Rigden. "I would if you insisted. But I hate the sound of it myself, for they treated her very badly on her marriage, and we never used to mention them from one year's end to another."

Moya pressed his hand, but not the point, though she was sorely tempted to do that too. She had even a sense of irritation at his caring to hide anything from her, but she was quick to see the unworthiness of this sentiment, and quicker to feel a remorse which demanded some sort of expression in order to restore complete self-approval. Yet she would not confess what had been (and still lingered) in her mind. So she fretted about the trifle in your true lover's fashion, and was silent until she hit upon a compromise.

"You know—if only anybody could!—how I would make up to you for all that you have lost, dearest. But nobody can. And I am full of the most diabolical faults—you can't imagine!"

And now she was all sincerity. But Rigden laughed outright.

"Tell me some of them," said he.

Moya hesitated; and did not confess her innate curiosity after all. She was still much too conscious of that blemish.

"I have a horrible temper," she said at length.

"I don't believe it."

"Ask Theodore."

"I certainly shouldn't believe him."

"Then wait and see."

"I will; and when I see it I'll show you what a real temper is like."

"Then—"

"Yes?"

"Well, I suppose I've had more attention than I deserve. So I suppose you might call me unreasonable—exacting—in fact, selfish!"

This was more vital; hence the hesitation on his part.

"When I do," said Rigden, solemnly, "you may send me about my business."

"It may be too late."

"Then we won't meet our troubles half-way," cried the young man, with virile common-sense. "Come! We love each other; that's good enough to go on with. And we've got the station to ourselves; didn't I work it well? So don't let's talk through our necks!"

The bush slang made the girl smile, but excitement had overstrung her finer nerves, and neither tone nor topic could she change at will.

"Shall we always love each other, darling?"

And there was the merest film of moisture upon the lovely eyes that were fixed so frankly upon his own.

"I can only answer for myself," he said, catching her mood. "I shall love you till I die."

"Whatever I do?"

"Even if you give me up."

"That's the one thing I shall never do, dearest."

"God bless you for saying it, Moya. If I knew what I have ever done or can do to deserve you!"

"Don't, dear ... you little dream ... but you will know me by and by."

"Please Heaven!"

And he leant and kissed her with all his might.

"Meanwhile—let us promise each other—there shall be no clouds between us while I am up here this week!"

"I'll kiss the Book on that."

"No shadows!"

"My dear child, why should there be?"

"There's Theodore—"

"Bother Theodore!"

"And then there are all those faults of mine."

"I don't believe in them. But if I did it would make no difference. It's not your qualities I'm in love with, Moya. It's yourself—so there's an end of it."

And an end there was, for about Rigden there was a crisp decisiveness which had the eventual advantage of a nature only less decided than his own. But it was strange that those should have been the last words.

Still stranger was it, as they sat together in a silence happier than their happiest speech, and as the lowering sun laid long shadows at their feet, that one of these came suddenly between them, and that it was not the shadow of pine-tree or verandah-post, but of a man.

CHAPTER II

INJURY

It was not Theodore, however. It was a man whom Moya was thankful not to have seen before. Nor was the face more familiar to Rigden himself, or less unlovely between the iron-grey bristles that wove a wiry mat from ear to ear, over a small head and massive jaws. For on attracting their attention the man lifted his wideawake, a trick so foreign to the normal bushman that Rigden's eyebrows were up from the beginning; yet he carried his swag as a swag should be carried; the outer blanket was the orthodox "bluey," duly faded; and the long and lazy stride that of the inveterate "sundowner."

"Eureka Station, I believe?" said the fellow, halting.

"That's the name," said Rigden.

"And are you the boss?"

"I am."

"Then Eureka it is!" cried the swagman, relieving himself of his swag, and heartily kicking it as it lay where he let it fall.

"But," said Rigden, smiling, "I didn't say I had any work for you, did I?"

"And I didn't ask for any work."

"Travellers' rations, eh? You'll have to wait till my storekeeper comes in. Go and camp in the travellers' hut."

Instead of a thank-you the man smiled—but only slightly—and shook his iron-grey head—but almost imperceptibly. Moya perceived it, however, and could not imagine why Rigden tolerated a demeanour which had struck her as insolent from the very first. She glanced from one man to the other. The smile broadened on the very unpleasant face of the tramp, making it wholly evil in the lady's eyes. So far from dismissing him, however, Rigden rose.

"Excuse me a few minutes," he said, not only briefly, but without even looking at Moya; and with a word to the interloper he led the way to the station store. This was one of the many independent buildings, and not the least substantial. The tramp followed Rigden, and in another moment a particularly solid door had closed behind the pair.

Moya felt at once hurt, aggrieved, and ashamed of her readiness to entertain any such feelings. But shame did not remove them. It was their first day together for two interminable months, and the afternoon was to have been their very very own. That was the recognised arrangement, and surely it was not too much to expect when one had come five hundred miles in the heat of January (most of them by coach) to see one's fiancé in one's future home. This afternoon, at least, they might have had to themselves. It should have been held inviolate. Yet he could desert her for the first uncleanly sundowner who came along! After first telling the man to wait, he must needs show his strength by giving in and attending to the creature himself, his devotion by leaving her alone on a verandah without another soul in sight or hearing! It might only be for the few minutes mentioned with such off-hand coolness. The slight was just the same.

Such was the first rush of this young lady's injured feelings and too readily embittered thoughts. They were more bitter, however, in form than in essence, for the notorious temper of the Australian Bethunes was seldom permitted a perfectly direct expression. They preferred the oblique ways of irony and sarcasm, and their minds ran in those curves. A little bitterness was in the blood, and Moya could not help being a Bethune.

But she had finer qualities than were rife—or at all events conspicuous—in the rank and file of her distinguished family. She had the quality of essential sweetness which excited their humorous contempt, and she was miraculously free from their innate and unparalleled cynicism. At her worst she had warm feelings, justly balanced by the faculty of cold expression. And at her best she was quick to see her faults and to deplore them; a candid and enthusiastic friend; staunch at your side, sincere to your face, loyal at all costs behind your back.

It was this loyalty that came to her rescue now: she stood suddenly self-convicted of a whole calendar of secret crime against the man whom she professed to love. Did she love him? Could she possibly love him, and so turn on him in an instant, even in her heart? Oh, yes, yes! She was a little fool, that was all; at least she hoped it was all. To think that her worst faults should hunt her up on the very heels of her frank confession of them! So in a few minutes sense prevailed over sensibility. And for a little all was well.

But these minutes mounted up by fives and then by tens. And the verandah was now filled to blindness and suffocation by the sunken sun. And there sat Moya Bethune, the admired of all the most admirable admirers elsewhere, baking and blinking in solitary martyrdom, while, with a grim and wilful obstinacy, she stoically waited the pleasure of a back-block overseer who preferred a disreputable tramp's society to hers!

The little fool in her was uppermost once more. There was perhaps some provocation now. Yet a little fool it indubitably was. She thought of freckles. Let them come. They would be his fault. Not that he would care.

Care!

And her short lip lifted in a peculiar smile; it was the war-smile of the Bethunes, and not beautiful in itself, but Moya it touched with such a piquant bitter-sweetness that some of her swains would anger her for that very look. Her teeth were white as the wing of the sulphur-crested cockatoo, and that look showed them as no other. Then there was the glitter it put into her eyes: they were often lovelier, but never quite so fine. And a sweet storm-light turned her skin from pale rose to glowing ivory, and the short lip would tremble one moment to set more unmercifully the next. Even so that those who loved and admired the milder Moya, feared and adored her thus.

But this Moya was seldom seen in Toorak, or, for that matter, anywhere else; and, of course, it was never to show itself any more, least of all at Eureka Station. Yet it did so this first, this very afternoon, though not all at once.

For the next thing that happened she took better than all that had gone before, though those were negative offences, and this was a positive affront.

It was when at last the store door opened, and Rigden went over to the kitchen for something steaming in a pannikin, and then to his room for something else. He passed once under Moya's nose, and once close beside her chair, but on each occasion without a look or a word.

"Something is worrying him," she thought. "Poor fellow!"

And for a space her heart softened. But it was no space to speak of; intensified curiosity cut it very short.

"Who can the horrid man be?"

The question paved the way to a new grievance and a new resolve.

"He ought to have told me. But he shall!"

Meanwhile the dividing door was once more shut; and now the better part of an hour had passed; and the only woman on the station (she might remain the only woman) had carried tea through the verandah and advised Moya to go indoors and begin. Moya declined. But no one ever sat in the sun up there. Moya said nothing; but at length gave so short an answer to so natural a question that Mrs. Duncan retreated with a very natural impression, false for the moment, but not for so many moments more.

For presently through the handful of pines, red-stemmed and resinous in the sunset, there came the jingle of bit and stirrup, to interrupt the unworthiest thoughts in which the insulted lady had yet indulged. She was thinking of much that she had missed in town by coming up-country in the height of the season; she was wishing herself back in Toorak. There she was somebody; in Toorak, in Melbourne, they would not dare to treat her thus.

Her fate was full of irony. There she could have had anybody, and, rightly or wrongly, she was aware of the fact. No other girl down there—or in Melbourne, for that matter—was at once a society belle, a general favourite, and a Bethune. The latter titles smacked indeed of the contradiction in terms, but their equal truth merely emphasised the altogether exceptional character of our heroine. That she was herself aware of it was not her fault. She had heard so much of her qualities for so many years. But all her life it had been impressed upon her mind that the Bethunes, as a family, were in a class by themselves in the southern hemisphere. In moments of chagrin, therefore, it was only natural that Moya should aggravate matters by remembering that she also was a Bethune.

A Bethune engaged to a bushman who dared to treat her thus!

Such was the pith and point of these discreditable reflections when the jingle of approaching horse put a sudden end to them. Moya looked up, expecting to see her brother, and instinctively donning a mask. She forgot it was in the buggy that Theodore had been got out of the way, and it was with sheer relief that her eyes lit upon a sergeant and a trooper of the New South Wales mounted police, with fluttering puggarees and twinkling accoutrements, and a black fellow riding bareback in the rear.

They reined up in front of the verandah.

"We want to see Mr. Rigden," said the sergeant, touching the shiny peak of his cap.

"Oh, indeed!"

"Is he about?"

Moya would not say, and pretended she could not. The sudden apparition of the police had filled her with apprehensions as wild as they were vague. The trooper had turned in his saddle to speak to the blackfellow, and Moya saw the great Government revolver at his hip. Even as she hesitated, however, the store door opened, and Rigden locked it behind him before sallying forth alone.

"Yes, here he is!" exclaimed Moya, and sat like a statue in her chair. Yet the pose of the statue was not wholly suggestive of cold indifference and utter unconcern.

"Glad to find you in, Mr. Rigden," said the sergeant. "We're having a little bit of sport, for once in a way."

"I congratulate you. What sort?" said Rigden.

"A man-hunt!"

And there were volumes of past boredom and of present zest in the sergeant's tone.

"That so?" said Rigden. "And who's the man?"

The sergeant glanced at the young lady. Rigden did the same. Their wishes with respect to her were only too obvious. Moya took the fiercer joy in disregarding them.

"I'd like to have a word with you in the store," said the sergeant.

"No, no!" said Rigden hastily. "Sergeant Harkness—Miss Bethune."

It was a cold little bow, despite this triumph.

"Miss Bethune will be interested," added Rigden grimly. "And she won't give anything away."

"Thank you," said Moya. And her tone made him stare.

Harkness touched his horse with the spurs, and rode up close to the verandah, on which Rigden himself now stood.

"Fact is," said he, "it oughtn't to get about among your men, or it's a guinea to a gooseberry they'll go harbouring him. But it's a joker who escaped from Darlinghurst a few days ago. And we've tracked him to your boundary—through your horse-paddock—to your home-paddock gate!"

Rigden glanced at Moya. Her eyes were on him. He knew it before he looked.

"Seen anything of him?" asked the sergeant inevitably.

"Not to my knowledge. What's he like?"

"Oldish. Stubby beard. Cropped head, of course. Grey as a coot."

"Height 5 ft. 11 in.," supplemented the trooper, reading from a paper; "'hair iron-grey, brown eyes, large thin nose, sallow complexion, very fierce-looking, slight build, but is a well-made man.'"

A dead silence followed; then Rigden spoke. Moya's eyes were still upon him, burning him, but he spoke without tremor, and with no more hesitation than was natural in the circumstances.

"No," he said, "I have seen no such man. No such man has been to me!"

"I was afraid of it," said Harkness. "Yet we tracked him to the boundary, every yard, and we got on his tracks again just now near the home-paddock gate. I bet he's camping somewhere within a couple of miles; we must have another look while it's light. Beastly lot of sand you have from the home-paddock gate right up to the house!"

"We're built upon a sandhill, you see," said Rigden, with a wry look into the heavy yellow yard: "one track's pretty much like another in here, eh, Billy?"

The black tracker shook a woolly pate.

"Too muchee damn allasame," said he. "Try again longa gate."

"Yes," said the sergeant, "and we'll bring him here for the night when we catch him. You could lend us your travellers' hut, I suppose?"

"Oh, yes."

"So long then, Mr. Rigden. Don't be surprised if you see us back to supper. I feel pretty warm."

And the sergeant used his spurs again, only to reign up suddenly and swing round in his saddle.

"Been about the place most of the afternoon?" he shouted.

"All the afternoon," replied Rigden; "between the store and this verandah."

"And you've had no travellers at all?"

"Not one."

"Well, never mind," cried the sergeant. "You shall have four for the night."

And the puggarees fluttered, and the stirrup irons jingled, out of sight and earshot, through the dark still pines, and so into a blood-red sunset.

CHAPTER III

INSULT

Rigden remained a minute at least (Moya knew it was five) gazing through the black trees into the red light beyond. That was so characteristic of him and his behaviour! Moya caught up the Australasian (at hand but untouched all this time) and pretended she could see to read. The rustle brought Rigden to the right about at last. Moya was deep in illegible advertisements. But the red light reached to her face.

Rigden came slowly to her side. She took no notice of him. His chair was as he had pushed it back an age ago; he drew it nearer than before, and sat down. Nor was this the end of his effrontery.

"Don't touch my hand, please!"

She would not even look at him. In a flash his face was slashed with lines, so deep you might have looked for them to fill with blood. There was plenty of blood beneath the skin. But he obeyed her promptly.

"I am sorry you were present just now," he remarked, as though nothing very tragical had happened. There was none the less an underlying note of tragedy which Moya entirely misconstrued.

"So am I," said she; and her voice nipped like a black frost.

"I wanted you to go, you know!" he reminded her.

"Do you really think it necessary to tell me that?"

All this time she was back in her now invisible advertisements. And her tone was becoming more and more worthy of a Bethune.

"I naturally didn't want you to hear me tell a lie," explained Rigden, with inconsistent honesty.

"On the contrary, I'm very glad to have heard it," rejoined Moya. "It's instructive, to say the least."

"It was necessary," said Rigden quietly.

"No doubt!"

"A lie sometimes is," he continued calmly. "You will probably agree with me there."

"Thank you," said Moya promptly; but no insinuation had been intended, no apology was offered, and Rigden proceeded as though no interruption had occurred.

"I am not good at them as a general rule," he confessed. "But just now I was determined to do my best. I suppose you would call it my worst!"

Moya elected not to call it anything.

"That poor fellow in the store—"

"I really don't care to know anything about him."

"—I simply couldn't do it," concluded Rigden expressively.

"Is he the man they want or not?"

The question came in one breath with the interruption, but with a change of tone so unguardedly complete that Rigden smiled openly. There was no answering smile from Moya. Her sense of humour, that saving grace of the Bethunes as a family, had deserted her as utterly as other graces of which she had more or less of a monopoly.

"Of course he's the man," said Rigden at once; but again there was the deeper trouble in his tone, the intrinsic trouble which mere results could not aggravate.

And this time Moya's perceptions were more acute. But by now pride had the upper hand of her. There was some extraordinary and mysterious reason for Rigden's conduct from beginning to end of this incident, or rather from the beginning to this present point, which was obviously not the end at all. Moya would have given almost anything to know what that reason was; the one thing that she would not give was the inch involved in asking the question in so many words. And Rigden in his innocence appreciated her delicacy in not asking.

"I can't explain," he began in rueful apology, and would have gone on to entreat her to trust him for once. But for some reason the words jammed. And meanwhile there was an opening which no Bethune could resist.

"Have I asked you for an explanation?"

"No. You've been awfully good about that. You're pretty rough on a fellow, all the same!"

"I don't think I am at all."

"Oh, yes, you are, Moya!"

For her tongue was beginning to hit him hard.

"You needn't raise your voice, Pelham, just because there's some one coming."

It was only the Eureka jackeroo (or "Colonial experiencer"), who had the hardest work on the station, and did it "for his tucker," but so badly as to justify Rigden in his bargain. It may here be mentioned that the manager's full name was Pelham Stanislaus Rigden; it was, however, a subconscious peculiarity of this couple never to address each other by a mere Christian name. Either they confined themselves to the personal pronoun, or they made use of expressions which may well be left upon their lovers' lips. But though scarcely aware of the habitual breach, they were mutually alive to the rare observance, which was perhaps the first thing to make Rigden realise the breadth and depth of his offence. It was with difficulty he could hold his tongue until the jackeroo had turned his horse adrift and betaken himself to the bachelors' hut euphemistically yclept "the barracks."

"What have I done," cried Rigden, in low tones, "besides lying as you heard? That I shall suffer for, to a pretty dead certainty. What else have I done?"

"Oh, nothing," said Moya impatiently, as though the subject bored her. In reality she was wondering and wondering why he should have run the very smallest risk for the sake of a runaway prisoner whom he had certainly pretended never to have seen before.

"But I can see there's something else," persisted Rigden. "What on earth is it, darling? After all I did not lie to you!"

"No," cried Moya, downright at last; "you only left me for two mortal hours alone on this verandah!"

Rigden sprang to his feet.

"Good heavens!" he cried; and little dreamed that he was doubling his enormity.

"So you were unaware of it, were you?"

"Quite!" he vowed naïvely.

"You had forgotten my existence, in fact? Your candour is too charming!"

His candour had already come home to Rigden, and he bitterly deplored it, but there was no retreat from the transparent truth. He therefore braced himself to stand or fall by what he had said, but meanwhile to defend it to the best of his ability.

"You don't know what an interview I had in yonder," he said, jerking a hand towards the store. "And the worst of it is that I can never tell you."

"Ah!"

"God forgive me for forgetting or neglecting you for a single instant!" Rigden exclaimed. "I can only assure you that when I left you I didn't mean to be gone five minutes. You will realise that what I eventually undertook to do for this wretched man made all the difference. It did put you out of my head for the moment; but you speak as though it were going to put you out of my life for all time!"

"For the sake of a man you pretended never to have seen before," murmured Moya, deftly assuming what she burned to know.

"It was no pretence. I didn't recognise him."

"But you do now," pronounced Moya, as one stating a perceptible fact.

"Yes," said Rigden, "I recognise him—now."

There was a pause. Moya broke it softly, a suspicion of sympathy in her voice.

"I am afraid he must have some hold over you."

"He has indeed," said Rigden bitterly; and next moment his heart was leaping, as a flame leaps before the last.

She who loved him was back at his side, she who had flouted him was no more. Her hot hands held both of his. Her quick breath beat upon his face. It was now nearly dark in the verandah, but there was just light enough for him to see the tears shining in her splendid eyes. Rigden was infinitely touched and troubled, but not by this alone. It was her voice that ran into his soul. She was imploring him to tell her all; there must be no secrets between them; let him but tell her the worst and she would stand by him, against all the world if need be, and no matter how bad the worst might be. She was no child. There was nothing he could not tell her, nothing she could not understand and forgive, except his silence. Silence and secrecy were the one unpardonable sin in her eyes. She would even help him to conceal that dreadful man, no matter what the underlying reason might be, or how much she might disagree with it, if only the reason were explained to her once and for all.

It was the one thing that Rigden would not explain.

He entreated her to trust him. His voice broke and the words failed him. But on the crucial point he was firm. And so was she.

"You said you were unreasonable and exacting," he groaned. "I didn't believe it. Now I see that it is true."

"But this is neither one nor the other," cried Moya. "Goodness! If I were never to exact more than your confidence! It's my right. If you refuse—"

"I do refuse it, in this instance, Moya."

"Then here's your ring!"

There was a wrench, a glitter, and something fell hot into his palm.

"I only hope you will think better of this," he said.

"Never!"

"I own that in many ways I have been quite in the wrong—"

"In every way!"

"There you are unreasonable again. I can't help it. I am doing what I honestly believe—"

His voice died away, for a whip was cracking in the darkness, with the muffled beat of unshod hoofs in the heavy sand. They sat together without a word, each waiting for the other to rise first; and thus Theodore found them, though Moya's dress was all he could descry at first.

"That you, Moya? Well, what price the bush? I've been shooting turkeys; they call it sport; but give me crows to-morrow! What, you there too, Rigden? Rum coincidence! Sorry I didn't see you sooner, old chap; but I'm not going to retract about the turkeys."

He disappeared in the direction of the barracks, and Moya held out her hand.

"Lend me that ring," she said. "There's no reason why we should give ourselves away to-night."

"I think the sooner the better," said Rigden.

But he returned the ring.

CHAPTER IV

BETHUNE OF THE HALL

Theodore Bethune was a young man of means, with the brains to add to them, and the energy to use his brains. As the eldest of his family he had inherited a special legacy in boyhood; had immediately taken himself away from the Church of England Grammar School, and booked his passage to London by an early boat. On the voyage he read the classics in his deck chair, asked copious questions in the smoking-room, and finally decided upon Cambridge as the theatre of his academical exploits.

Jesus was at that time the College most favoured by Australasian youth: this was quite enough for Theodore Bethune. He ultimately selected Trinity Hall, as appearing to him to offer the distinction of Trinity without its cosmopolitan flavour, and a legal instead of an athletic tradition. In due course he took as good a degree as he required, and proceeded to be called at the English bar before returning to practice in Melbourne. In connection with his university life he had two or three original boasts: he had never been seen intoxicated, never played any game, and only once investigated Fenner's (to watch the Australians). On the other hand, he had added appreciably to his income by intelligent betting on Newmarket course.

Temperament, character, and attainment seemed to have combined to produce the perfect barrister in Theodore Bethune, who was infinitely critical but himself impervious to criticism, while possessed of a capital gift of insolence and a face of triple brass. The man, however, was not so perfect; even the gentleman may exhibit certain flaws. Of these one of his sisters had latterly become very conscious; but they came out as a boon to her on the second evening of this visit to Eureka Station, New South Wales.

For in conversation Bethune was what even he would formerly have called "a terror," an epithet which he still endeavoured to deserve, though he no longer made use of it himself. Captious, cocksure, omniscient, he revelled in the uses of raillery and of repartee. Nothing pleased him more than to combat the pet theories of persons whom he had no occasion to conciliate. He could take any side on any question, as became the profession he never ceased from practising. He destroyed illusions as other men destroy game, and seldom made a new acquaintance without securing a fair bag. Better traits were a playful fancy and an essential geniality which suggested more of mischief than of malice in the real man; the pose, however, was that of uncompromising and heartless critic of every creature of his acquaintance, and every country in which he had set foot.

The first night he had behaved very well. Moya had made him promise that he would not be openly critical for twenty-four hours. He had kept his word like a man and a martyr. The second night was different. Theodore was unmuzzled. And both Moya and Rigden were thankful in their hearts.

Sir Oracle scarce knew where to begin. There were the turkeys which a child could have hit with a pop-gun; there were the emus which the Queen's Prizeman could not have brought down with his Lee-Metford. But Theodore had discovered that there was no medium in the bush. Look at the heat! He had been through the Red Sea at its worst, but it had not fetched the skin from his hands as this one day in Riverina. Riverina, forsooth! Where were their rivers? Lucus a non lucendo.

The storekeeper winked; he was a humorist himself, of a lower order.

"No good coming it in Greek up here, mister."

The jackeroo was the storekeeper's hourly butt. The jackeroo was a new chum who had done pretty badly at his public school, and was going to do worse in the bush, but he still knew Latin from Greek when he heard it, and he perceived his chance of scoring off the storekeeper.

"Greek is good," said the jackeroo. "Greek is great!"

"Ah, now we have it!" cried the storekeeper, who was a stout young man with bulbous eyes, and all the sly glances of the low comedian. "'Tis the voice of the scholard, I heard him explain! He comes from Rugby, Mr. Bethune; hasn't he told you yet? Calls himself an Old Rug—sure it isn't a plaid-shawl, Ives? Oh, you needn't put on side because you can draft Greek from Latin!"

Ives the jackeroo, a weak youth wearing spectacles, had put on nothing but the long-suffering smile with which he was in the habit of receiving the storekeeper's grape-shot. He said no more, however, and a brief but disdainful silence on the part of Bethune made an awkward pause which Rigden broke heroically. Hitherto but little talking had been required of him or of Moya. The aggressive Theodore had been their unwitting friend, and he stood them in better stead than ever when the young men adjourned to smoke on the verandah.

This was the time when the engaged couple would naturally have disappeared; they had duly done so the previous evening; to-night they merely sat apart, out of range of the lamp, and the young men galled them both by never glancing their way. Nothing had been noticed yet; nor indeed was there anything remarkable in their silence after so long a day spent in each other's exclusive society. From time to time, however, they made a little talk to save appearances which were incriminating only in their own minds; and all the time their eyes rested together upon the black stack of logs and corrugated iron which was the store.

Once the storekeeper approached with discreet deliberation.

"I've lost my key of the store, Mr. Rigden; may I borrow yours?"

"It's I who've lost mine, Spicer, so I took yours from your room. No, don't bother about your books to-night; don't go over there again. Look after Mr. Bethune."

He turned to Moya when the youth was gone.

"One lie makes many," he muttered grimly.

There was no reply.

Meanwhile Bethune was in his element, with an audience of two bound to listen to him by the bond of a couple of his best cigars, and with just enough of crude retaliation from the storekeeper to act as a blunt cutlass to Theodore's rapier. The table with the lamp was at the latter's elbow, and the rays fell full upon the long succesful nose and the unwavering mouth of an otherwise rather ordinary legal countenance. There was plenty of animation in the face, however, and enough of the devil to redeem a good deal of the prig. The lamp also made the most of a gleaming shirt-front; for Theodore insisted on dressing ("for my own comfort, purely,") even in the wilderness, where black coats were good enough for the other young men, and where Mora herself wore a high blouse.

"But there's nothing to be actually ashamed of in an illusion or two," the jackeroo was being assured, "especially at your age. I've had them myself, and may have one or two about me still. You only know it when you lose them, and my faith in myself has been rudely shattered. I've shed one thundering big illusion since I've been up here."

The Rugby boy was not following; he had but expressed a sufficiently real regret at not having gone up to Cambridge himself; and he was wondering whether he should regret it the less in future for what this Cambridge man had to say upon the subject. On the whole it did not reconcile him to the university of the bush, and for a little he had a deaf ear for the conversation. A question had been asked and answered ere he recovered the thread.

"Oh, go on," said the storekeeper. "Give the back-blocks a rest, Bethune!"

"I certainly shall, Mr. Spicer," rejoined Theodore, with the least possible emphasis on the prefix, "once I shake their infernal dust from my shoes. Not that I'd mind the dust if there was anything to do in it. Of course this sort of thing's luxury," he had the grace to interject; "in fact, it's far too luxurious for me. One rather likes to rough it when one comes so far. Anything for some excitement, some romance, something one can't get nearer home!"

"Well, you can't get this," said the loyal storekeeper.

"I never was at a loss for moonlight," observed Theodore, "when there happened to be a moon. There are verandahs in Toorak."

Spicer lowered his voice.

"There was a man once shot dead in this one. Bushrangers!"

"When was that?"

"Oh, well, it was before my time."

"Ten years ago?"

"Ten to twenty, I suppose."

"Ten to twenty! Why, my good fellow, there was a blackfellows' camp in Collins Street, twenty years ago! Corrobborees, and all that, where the trams run now."

"I'm hanged if there were," rejoined Spicer warmly. "Not twenty years ago, no, nor yet thirty!"

"Say forty if it makes you happy. It doesn't affect my argument. You don't expect me to bolt out of this verandah because some poor devil painted it red before I was breeched? What shall it profit us that there were bushrangers once upon a time, and blacks before the bushrangers? The point is that they're both about as extinct as the plesiosaurus—"

"Kill whose cat?" interposed the storekeeper in a burst of his peculiar brand of badinage. "He's coming it again, Ives; you'll have another chance of showing off, old travelling-rug!"

"And all you've got to offer one instead," concluded Bethune, "besides the subtleties of your own humour, is a so-called turkey the size of a haystack, that'll ram its beak down your gun-barrel if you wait long enough."

The Rugbeian laughed outright, and Spicer gained time by insulting him while he rummaged his big head for a retort worthy of Bethune; it was worthier of himself when it came.

"You want adventure, do you? I know the place for you, and its within ten miles of where you sit. Blind Man's Block!"

"Reminds one of the Tower," yawned Bethune.

"It'll remind you of your sins if ever you get bushed in it! Ten by ten of abandoned beastliness; not a hoof or a drop between the four fences; only scrub, and scrub, and scrub of the very worst. Mallee and porcupine—porcupine and mallee. But you go and sample it; only don't get too far in from the fence. If you do you may turn up your toes; and you won't be the first or the last to turn 'em up in Blind Man's Block."

"What of?" asked Bethune sceptically.

"Thirst," said Spicer; "thirst and hunger, but chiefly thirst."

"In fenced country?"

"It's ten miles between the fences, and not a drop of water, nor the trace of a track. It's abandoned country, I'm telling you."

"But you could never be more than five miles from a fence; surely you could hit one or other of them and follow it up?"

"Could you?" said the storekeeper. "Well, you try it, and let me know! Try it on horseback, and you'll see what it's like to strike a straight line through mallee and porcupine; and after that, if you're still hard up for an adventure, just you try it on foot."

"Don't you, Theodore," advised Rigden from his chair. "I'm not keen on turning out all hands to look for you, old chap."

"But is the place really as bad as all that?" inquired Moya, following him into the conversation for the look of the thing.

"Worse," said Rigden, and leaned forward, silent. In another moment he had risen, walked to the end of the verandah, and returned as far as Bethune's chair. "Sure you want an adventure, Theodore? Because the Assyrians are coming down in the shape of the mounted police, and it's the second time they've been here to-day. Looks fishy, doesn't it?"

Listening, they heard the thin staccato jingle whose first and tiniest tinkle had been caught by Rigden; then with one accord the party rose, and gathered at the end of the verandah, whence the three black horsemen could be seen ambling into larger sizes, among the tussocks of blue-bush, between the station and the rising moon.

"What do they want?" idly inquired Bethune.

"A runaway convict," said Rigden, quietly.

"No!" cried Spicer.

"Is it a fact?" asked Ives, turning instinctively to Miss Bethune.

"I believe so," replied Moya, with notable indifference.

"Then why on earth have you been keeping it dark, both of you?" demanded Bethune, and he favoured the engaged couple with a scrutiny too keen for one of them. Moya's eyes fell. But Rigden was equal to the occasion.

"Because the police don't want it to get about. That's why," said he shortly.

And Moya admired his resource until she had time to think; then it revolted her as much as all the rest. But meanwhile the riders were dismounting in the moonlight. Rigden went out to meet them, and forthwith disappeared with Harkness among the pines.

"No luck at all," growled the sergeant. "We're clean off the scent, and it licks me how he gave you such a wide berth and us the slip. We can't have been that far behind him. None of the other gentlemen came across him, I suppose?"

"As a matter of fact I've only just mentioned it to them," replied Rigden, rather lamely. "I thought I'd leave it till you came back. You seemed not to want it to get about, you know."

"No more I do—for lots of reasons. I mean to take the devil, alive or dead, and yet I don't want anybody else to take him! Sounds well, doesn't it? Yet I bet you'd feel the same in my place—if you knew who he was!"

Rigden stood mute.

"You won't cut me out for the reward, Mr. Rigden, if I tell you who it is, between ourselves? You needn't answer: of course you won't. Well—then—it's good old Bovill the bushranger!" And the sergeant's face shone like the silver buttons of the sergeant's tunic.

"Captain Bovill!" gasped Rigden, but only because he felt obliged to gasp something.

"Not so loud, man!" implored the sergeant, who had sunk his own voice to the veriest whisper. "Yes—yes—that's the gentleman. None other! Incredible, isn't it? Of course it wasn't Darlinghurst he escaped from, but Pentridge; only I thought you'd guess if I said; it's been in the papers some days."

"We get ours very late, and haven't always time to read them then. I knew nothing about it."

"Well, then, you knew about as much as is known in Victoria from that day to this. The police down there have lost their end of the thread, and it was my great luck to pick it up again by the merest chance last week. I'll tell you about that another time. But you understand what it would mean to me?"

"Rather!"

"To land him more or less single-handed!"

"I won't tell a soul."

"And don't you go and take the man himself behind my back, Mr. Rigden!" the policeman was obliged to add, with such jocularity as men feign in their deadliest earnest.

But Rigden's laugh was genuine and involuntary.

"I can safely promise that I won't do that," said he. "But ask the other fellows if they've seen the kind of man you describe; if they haven't, no harm done."

The unprofitable inquiry was conducted in Moya's presence, who abruptly disappeared, unable to bear any more and still hold her peace. Thereupon Rigden breathed more freely, and offered supper with an improving grace; the very tracker was included in the invitation, which was accepted with the frank alacrity of famished men.

"And it's not the last demand we shall have to make on you," said Harkness, as he washed in Rigden's room; "we've ridden our cattle off their legs since we were here in the afternoon. We must hark back on our own tracks first thing in the morning. Beds or bunks we shall want for the night, and fresh horses for an early start."

Rigden thought a moment.

"By all means, if you can stand the travellers' hut. It's empty, but in here we're rather full. As for horses, I've the very three for you. I'll run 'em up myself."

The storekeeper came to him as he was pulling on his boots. He was not a conspicuously attractive young man, but he had one huge merit. His devotion to Rigden was quite extraordinary.

"Why not let one of us run up those horses, sir?"

"One of you! I like that. Give us those spurs."

"Well, of course I meant myself, Mr. Rigden. The new chum wouldn't be much use."

"I'm not sure that you'd be much better. You don't know the paddocks as I know them, nor the mokes either. Nobody does, for that matter. But I don't want the men to get wind of this to-night."

"I'll see that they don't, Mr. Rigden."

"Now I'm ready, and I'll be twice as quick as anybody else. What's the time, Spicer?"

"Just on ten."

"Well, I'll be back by eleven. Now go in and see they've got everything they want, and take Mr. Bethune in with you for a drink. That's your billet for to-night, Spicer; you've got to play my part and leave the store to take care of itself. Now I'm off."

But it was some minutes before he proceeded beyond the horse-yard; indeed, he loitered there, though the jackeroo had the night-horse ready saddled, until Theodore had accepted the storekeeper's invitation, and the verandah was empty at last.

"Hang it! I'll have my dust-coat," he cried when about to mount. "Hold him while I run back to the barracks."

"Can't I go for you, sir?"

"No, you can't."

And the Rugby boy thought wistfully of Cambridge while Rigden was gone; for he was an absent-minded youth, who did not even notice how the pockets of the dust-coat bulged when Rigden returned.

Only Moya, from her dark but open door on that same verandah, had seen the manager slip from the barracks over to the store, and remain there some minutes, with the door shut and the key inside, before creeping stealthily out and once more locking the door behind him.

CHAPTER V

A RED HERRING

Rigden cantered to the horse-paddock gate, and on and on along the beaten track which intersected that enclosure, and which led ultimately to a wool-shed pitched further from the head-station than wool-shed ever was before or since. Rigden rode as though he were on his way thither; he certainly had not the appearance of a man come to cut out horses in a horse-paddock. His stock-whip was added to the bulging contents of the dust-coat pockets, instead of being ready as a lance in rest. The rider looked neither right nor left as he rode. He passed a mob of horses in the moonlight, not without seeing them, but without a second glance.

Suddenly he left the track at a tangent; but there was no symptom of the sudden thought. Rigden sat loosely in his saddle, careless but alert, a man who knew every inch of the country, and his own mind to an irreducible nicety. A clump of box rose in his path; a round-shot would have cut through quicker, but not more unerringly. Rigden came out on the edge of a chain of clay-pans, hard-baked by the sun, and shining under the moon like so many water-holes.

Rigden rode a little way upon the nearest hard, smooth surface; then he pulled up, and, looking back, could see scarcely any trace of his horse's hoofs. He now flung a leg across the saddle, and sat as the ladies while his quiet beast stood like bronze. A night-horse is ex officio a quiet beast.

Rigden wondered whether any man had ever before changed his boots on horseback. When he proceeded it was afoot, with his arm through the reins, and the pockets of the dust-coat bulging more than ever. From his walk it was manifest that the new shoes pinched.

But they left no print unless he stamped with all his might. And that was a very painful process. Rigden schooled himself to endure it, however, and repeated the torture two or three times on his way across the clay-pans. On such occasions the night-horse was made to halt (while the stamping was done under its nose) and to pirouette in fashion that must have astonished the modest animal almost as much as each fresh inspiration astonished Rigden himself.

On the sandy ground beyond he merely led the horse until a fence was reached. Here some minutes were spent, not only in strapping down the wires and coaxing the night-horse over, but in some little deliberation which ended in the making of mock footprints with his own boots, without, however, putting them on. Rigden had still another mile to do in the tight shoes for this his sin. It brought him to the pouting lips of a tank (so called) where the moon shone in a mirror of still water framed in slime. Here he gave his horse a drink, and, remounting, changed his boots once more. A sharp canter brought him back to the fence; it was crossed as before; the right horses were discovered and cut out with the speed and precision of a master bushman; and at half-past eleven exactly the thunder of their hoofs and the musketry of Rigden's stock-whip were heard together in the barracks, where the rest had gathered for a final pipe.

"Good time," said the sergeant, who was seated with his subordinate on the storekeeper's bed.

"Not for him," said Spicer. "He said he'd be back by eleven. He's generally better than his word."

"A really good man at his work—what?"

Bethune had been offered the only chair, and was not altogether pleased with himself for having accepted it. It was rather a menagerie, this storekeeper's room, with these policemen smoking their rank tobacco. Theodore had offered them his cigars, to put an end to the reek, but his offer had come too late. He hardly knew why he remained; not even to himself would he admit his anxiety to know what was going to happen next. A criminal case! It would teach him nothing; he never touched criminal work; none of your obvious law and vulgar human interest for him.

"Good man?" echoed Spicer the loyal. "One of the best on God's earth; one of the straightest that ever stepped. Don't you make any mistake about that, Bethune! I've known him longer than you."

The testimonial was superfluous in its warmth and fulness, yet not uncalled for if Bethune's tone were taken seriously. It was, however, merely the tone in which that captious critic was accustomed to refer to the bulk of humanity; indeed, it was complimentary for him. Before more could be added, "the straightest man that ever stepped" had entered, looking the part. His step was crisp and confident; there was a lively light in his eye.

"Have a job to find them?" inquired his champion.

"Well," said Rigden, "I found something else first."

"The man?" they all cried as one.

"No, not the man," said Rigden smiling. "Where's your tracker, sergeant?"

"Put him in your travellers' hut, Mr. Rigden."

"Quite right. I only wanted to ask him something, but I dare say you can tell me as well. Get that track pretty plain before you lost it this afternoon?"

"Plain as a pikestaff, didn't we?" said the sergeant to his sub.

"My oath!" asseverated the trooper, who was a man of few words.

"Notice any peculiarity about it, Harkness?"

"Yes," said the sergeant.

"What?" pursued Rigden.

"That," said Harkness; and he produced a worn heel torn from its sole and uppers.

"Exactly," said Rigden, nodding.

The sergeant sprang from the bed.

"Have you struck his tracks?"

"I won't say that," said Rigden. "All I undertake is to show you a distinct track with no left heel to it all down the line. No, I won't shake hands on it. It may lead to nothing."

All was now excitement in the small and smoky bedroom. The jackeroo had appeared on the scene from his own room, to which his sensitive soul ever banished him betimes. All were on their feet but Bethune, who retained the only chair, but with eyes like half-sheathed blades, and head at full-cock.

"Did you follow it up?" asked the sergeant.

"Yes, a bit."

"Where did you strike it?"

"I'll tell you what: you shall be escorted to the spot."

"Um!" said the sergeant; "not by all hands, I hope?"

"By Mr. Spicer and nobody else. I'd come myself, only I've found other fish to fry. Look here, Spicer," continued Rigden, clapping the storekeeper on the shoulder; "you know the clay-pans in the horse-paddock? Well, you'll see my tracks there, and you'd better follow them; there are just one or two of the others; but on the soft ground you'll see the one as plain as the other. You'll have to cross the fence into Butcher-boy; you'll see where I crossed it. That's our killing-sheep paddock, Harkness; think your man could kill and eat a sheep?"

"I could kill and eat you," said the sergeant cordially, "for the turn you've done me."

"Thanks; but you wait and see how it pans out. All I guarantee is that the tracks are there; how far they go is another matter. I only followed them myself as far as the tank in Butcher-boy. And that reminds me: there'll be a big muster to-morrow, Spicer. The tank in Butcher-boy's as low as low; the Big Bushy tanks always go one worse; we'll muster Big Bushy to-morrow, whether or no. I've been meaning to do it for some time. Besides, it'll give you all the freer hand for those tracks, sergeant: we shall be miles apart."

"That's all right," said the sergeant. "But I should have liked to get on them to-night."

"The moon's pretty low."

Harkness looked out.

"You're right," he said. "We'll give it best till morning. Come, mate, let's spell it while we can."

The rest separated forthwith. Bethune bade his future brother-in-law good-night without congratulation or even comment on the discovery of the tracks. Rigden lingered a moment with his lieutenants, and then remarked that he had left his coat in the harness-room; he would go and fetch it, and might be late, as he had letters to write for the mail.

"Can't I get the coat, sir?" asked the willing jackeroo.

Rigden turned upon him with unique irritation.

"No, you can't! You can go to bed and be jolly well up in time to do your part to-morrow! It's you I am studying, my good fellow," he made shift to add in a kindlier tone; "you can't expect to do your work unless you get your sleep. And I want you to round up every hoof in the horse-paddock by sunrise, and after that every man in the hut!"

CHAPTER VI

BELOW ZERO

"May I come in?"

It was her brother at Moya's door, and he began to believe she must be asleep after all. Theodore felt aggrieved; he wanted speech with Moya before he went to bed. He was about to knock again when the door was opened without a word. There was no light in the room. Yet the girl stood fully dressed in the last level rays of the moon. And she had been crying.

"Moya!"

"What do you want?"

"Only to speak to you."

"What about?"

"Yourself, to begin with. What's the trouble, my dear girl?"

He had entered in spite of her, and yet she was not really sorry that he had come. She had suffered so much in silence that it would be relief to speak about anything to anybody. Theodore was the last person in whom she could or would confide. But there was something comfortable in his presence just there and then. She could tell him a little, if she could not tell him all; and he could tell her something in return.

She heard him at his match-box, and shut the door herself as he lit the candles.

"Don't speak loud, then," said Moya. "I—I'd rather they didn't hear us—putting our heads together."

"No fear. We've got the main building to ourselves, you and I. Rather considerate of Rigden, that."

Indeed it was the best parlour that had been prepared for Moya, for in your southern summers the best parlour of all is the shadiest verandah. Theodore took to the sofa and a cigarette.

"Do you mind?" he said. "Then do please tell me what's the matter with you, Moya!"

"Oh, can't you see? I'm so unhappy!"

Her eyes had filled, but his next words dried them.

"Had a row with Rigden?"

And he was leaning forward without his cigarette.

Moya hated him.

"Is that all that occurs to you?" she asked cuttingly. "I'm sorry to disappoint you, I'm sure! I should have thought even you could have seen there was enough to make one unhappy, without the consummation you so devoutly—"

"Good, Moya! That's all right," said her brother, as he might have complimented her across the net at lawn-tennis.

"It's quite unpleasant enough," continued Moya, with spirit, "without your making it worse. The police in possession, and a runaway convict goodness knows where!"

"I agree," said Theodore. "It is unpleasant. I wonder where the beggar can be?"

"It's no use asking me," said Moya; for the note of interrogation had been in his voice.

"You didn't see any suspicious-looking loafers, I suppose? I mean this afternoon."

"How could I? I was with Pelham all the time."

She would never marry him, never! That was no reason why she should give him away. She would never marry a man with discreditable secrets which she might not share, not because they were discreditable, but for the other reason. Yet she must be a humbug for his sake! Moya felt a well-known eye upon her, felt her face bathed in fire; luckily her explanation itself might account for that, and she had the wit to see this in time.

"I mean," she stammered, "one was on the verandah all the afternoon. Nobody could have come without our seeing them."

"I don't know about that. Love is blind!"

His tone carried relief to Moya. The irony was characteristic, normal. It struck her as incompatible with any strong suspicion. But the ground was dangerous all the same.

"If we are made uncomfortable," said Moya, shifting it, "what must it be for Pelham! It's on his account I feel so miserable."

And she spoke the truth; indeed, a truism; but she would be still more miserable if she married him. She would never marry a man—the haunting sentence went for once unfinished. Theodore was favouring her with a peculiar scrutiny whose import she knew of old. She was on her guard just in time.

"You haven't heard the latest development, I suppose?"

"Has there been something fresh since I came away?"

And even Theodore did not know that she was holding her breath.

"Something as fresh as paint," said he dryly. "Rigden thinks he's got on the fellow's tracks."

Moya had braced herself against any sudden betrayal of alarm; she was less proof against the inrush of a new contempt for her lover.

"You don't mean it!" she cried with indignation.

"Why not?" asked Theodore blandly.

"Oh, nothing. Only it's pretty disgraceful—on the part of the police, I mean—that they should spend hours looking for what a mere amateur finds at once!"

The brother peeped at her from lowered lids. He was admiring her resource.

"I agree," he said slowly, "if—our friend is right."

"Whom do you mean?" inquired Moya, up in arms on the instant.

"Rigden, of course."

"So you think he may be mistaken about the tracks, do you?"

"I think it's possible."

"You know a lot about such things yourself, of course! You have a wide experience of the bush, haven't you? What do the police think?"

"They're leaving it till the morning. They hope for the best."

"So everybody is pleased except my brilliant brother! I want to know why—I want to know more about these tracks."

He told her more with unruffled mien; he rather enjoyed her sarcasm; it both justified and stimulated his own. Sarcasm he held to be the salt of intercourse. It was certainly a game at which two Bethunes could always play.

"But we shall see in the morning," concluded Theodore. "The heathen is to be put upon the scent at dawn; if he passes it, well and good."

"Meanwhile you don't?"

"No, I'm hanged if I do," said Theodore, bluntly.

"Because you haven't been to see?"

Theodore smiled.

"Because you wouldn't know a man's track from a monkey's if you went?"

Theodore laughed.

"Why drag in Darwin, my dear girl? No, I've not been to look, and yet I'm not convinced. I just have my doubts, and a reason or so for them; then I haven't your admirable ground of belief in the infallibility of our host's judgment. He may be mistaken. Mistakes do get made by moonlight. Let's put it at that."

But Moya knew that he was not putting it at that in his mind, and she made up hers to learn the worst of his suspicions.

"If the tracks are not his, whose are they?" she demanded, as though it mattered. "If the creature is not somewhere about the run, where is he?"

And this did matter.

"If you ask me," said Theodore, with great gravity for him, "I should say that he was within a few yards of us all the time!"

"A few yards?"

"I should say," repeated Theodore, "that he was somewhere about the homestead, not the run. And you know perfectly well that you agree!"

"I?"

She jumped up in a fury.

"How dare you say that to me? How dare you, Theodore?"

"My dear Moya, I'm at a loss to understand you!" and his eyebrows underlined the words into largest capitals. "How on earth have I offended? I'm quite sure that you have the same suspicion—not to call it fear—that I entertain myself. If not, why be in such a state? Why not go to bed and to sleep like a rational person? I confess I don't feel like doing so myself—with the chance of waking up to find an escaped criminal on your chest. I prefer to sit up and keep watch. I'm convinced he's somewhere about;

all these huts afford far better cover than the open paddocks, bless you! He could easily have slipped among them without either of you seeing him, and the chances are he has."

"If you think that," said Moya, "why didn't you suggest it?"

"I did—to Rigden. Wouldn't listen to me; so, of course, I can't expect you to be so disloyal as to do so either."

But Moya had no more of that kind of fight in her. "So you intend to sit up and watch?" was her sole rejoinder.

"I do."

"Then so do I!"

Theodore looked dubious, but only for an instant.

"You begin to think there may be something in my theory?"

"I think there—may be."

"Then I'll tell you more!" exclaimed Theodore with decision: "I believe the fellow's over yonder in that store!"

His eyes were waiting for her face to change. But it changed very little. Moya was beginning to wonder whether her terrible brother did not already know all. One moment she thought he did, the next that he did not; indifference was creeping over her with the long-drawn strain of the situation. What did it matter if he did know? It would make no difference between her and Pelham. That was at an end, in any case; all that was at an end for ever.

Meanwhile she humoured Theodore just a little, particularly in the matter of her sitting up. He begged her not to do so, and she feigned consent. One of his objects in sitting up himself was to secure her safety. He might be wrong in all his conjectures, and Rigden might be right. Theodore was none the less virtuously determined not to give a chance away.

"And if I am right I'll nab him the moment he shows his nose; and the credit will belong to your humble brother. It isn't as if I hadn't mentioned my general ideas to Rigden; otherwise it might be rather much to take upon one's self; but as it is I have no scruples. If nothing happens, I've simply been sleeping on the verandah, because it's cooler there, and that long chair's as good as any bed. Do you mind doing something for me, Moya?"

"What is it?"

"My room's at the back, as you know; do you mind keeping a look-out while I go round and get into my pyjamas?"

"No, I don't mind."

"Particularly on the store, you know."

"Yes, I know."

"If anything happens come straight to me, but as quietly as possible."

"Very well."

"I mean if you see anybody."

"Yes."

"But I shan't be many minutes."

And he was gone.

At last!

Moya flung herself upon the bed, and lay for a few seconds with closed eyes. Her forehead was wondrous white; the fine eyebrows and the long lashes seemed suddenly to have gone black; the girl was fainting under the triple strain of fear and shame and outraged love. Yes, she was in love, but she would never marry him. Never! It was the irony of her fate to love a man whom she would rather die than marry, after this! Yet she loved him none the less; that was the last humiliation of women whom she had scorned all her days for this very thing, only to become one of them in the end.

But she at least would never marry the man she loved and yet despised. That would be the only difference, yet a fairly essential one. And now her strength was renewed with her resolve, so that she was up and doing within the few seconds aforesaid; her first act was to blow out the candle; her next, to open the door an inch and to take her stand at the opening.

Nor was she much too soon. It was as though Rigden had been only waiting for her light to go out. Within a minute he appeared in the sandy space between the main building and the store. He was again wearing the yellow silk dust-coat of which enough has been heard; it was almost all that could be seen of him in the real darkness which had fallen with the setting of the moon.

Moya heard his key in the heavy door opposite. Should she tell him of Theodore's suspicions, or should she not? While she hesitated, he let himself in, took out the key, and once more locked the door behind him. Next moment a thread of light appeared upon the threshold; and, too late, Moya repented her indecision.

Theodore would return, and then—

But for once he was singularly slow; minute followed minute, and there was neither sign nor sound of him.

And presently the store door opened once more; the figure in the dust-coat emerged as it had entered; and vanished as it had appeared, in the direction of the horse-yard.

Once more the door was shut; but, once more, that thread of incriminating light burnt like a red-hot wire beneath. And this time Moya could not see it burn: the red-hot wire had entered her soul. Theodore had been so long, he might be longer; risk it she must, and take the consequences. Two steps carried her across the verandah; lighter she had never taken in a ball-room, where her reputation was that of a feather. Once in the kindly sand, however, she ran desperately, madly, to the horse-yard. And she was just in time to hear the dying beat of a horse's canter into infinity.

Then she must inform the wretch himself, the runaway ruffian in the store! One sob came, and then this quick resolve.

She gained the store, panting; and instinctively tried the door before knocking. To her amazement and alarm it was open. She stood confounded on the threshold, and a head bending over the desk, under the lamp, behind the counter, was suddenly transformed into a face. And it was not the runaway at all; it was Rigden himself!

"I saw you come out!" she gasped, past recrimination, past anger, past memory itself in the semi-insensibility of over-whelming surprise. He looked at her very gravely across the desk.

"No, that was the man who has wrecked my life," he said. "I've got him through them at last, I do believe."

And his eyes flashed their unworthy triumph.

"You could actually give him your horse!"

"I wish I could. It would be missed in a minute. No, he's only just to run the gauntlet on it, and I shall find it at the first gate. But what is it, Moya? You came for something?" and he was a miserable man once more.

"I'm ashamed to say why I came—but I will!" cried Moya in a low voice. "I did not want you to be found out through my own brother. He suspected the man was in here—I don't know why. He was going to watch the store all night, and I was watching it for him while he changed, and the light under the door—"

Rigden held up his hand.

"Hush!" he said. "Here is your brother."

Theodore was more than decent; he was positively gorgeous in striped and tasselled silk. He stood in the doorway with expressive eyebrows and eloquent nostrils, looking from Moya to Rigden until his gaze settled upon the latter. It was almost an innocuous gaze by then.

"So it was you in here," he said. Rigden nodded. "Do you know who I was ass enough to think it was?" continued Theodore, using a word which Moya had never heard him apply to himself before, even in fun. "Has Moya told you?"

"She has."

"I saw the light," said Moya, in elliptical explanation. Theodore continued to address his host.

"I oughtn't to have interfered," he said, with a humility which was already arousing Moya's suspicions. "I should have minded my own business, Rigden, and I apologise. I'd got it into my head—I can't tell you why. Will you forgive me? And have you any more whisky?"

"I've nothing to forgive," said Rigden, sincerely enough. "But a drink we'll have; that's an excellent idea!"

But the counter was between them, and Theodore was the first to leave the store; but on the threshold he stopped, and just turned to Moya for an instant.

"By the way, you didn't see anybody else, I suppose?" said he.

There was an instant's pause. Then Moya committed her sin.

"Of course I didn't," were the words.

Theodore strolled over to the verandah. Moya waited behind as in devotion while Rigden locked that fatal door for the last time.

"You see what you've brought me to!" she hissed. "But don't think it's because I care a bit what happens to you—once I'm gone. And I hate you for it—and I always shall!"

"Thank you," he said.

And that was all.

CHAPTER VII

A CAVALIER

Moya went to bed like one already in a dream. She smiled when she realised what she was doing; there would be no sleep for her that night. Yet she went through with the empty form, even to putting out the light to rest her aching eyes. And in five minutes her troubles ceased for as many hours; she had passed that pitch of excitement which is another name for insomnia; she had reached the stage of sheer exhaustion, and she reaped the recompense.

Spurred feet treading gingerly nevertheless awoke her towards dawn. It was a bitter awakening. Further sleep was impossible, further rest intolerable; besides, something must be done at once. It was an ordeal to face, but sooner or later Theodore must be told, and then—good-bye! Obviously the sooner the better, since the thing was settled between the two whom it concerned; and Moya had the temperament which prefers to precipitate the absolutely inevitable; but temperament for once was not her lord. It was too hard!

Character came to the rescue. It must be done. And Moya dressed by candle-light with a craven but a resolute heart.

Meanwhile the cautious footsteps and the low voices died away; and the girl found a bare verandah, chill and silent as a vault in the twilight of early morning. A lamp was burning in the dining-room, but the chairs were pushed back, crusts left, and tea-cups half full. The teapot felt quite heavy; and Moya took a cup and a bite before going to see whether Theodore was awake. If not, she must wake him, for she could not wait. But his room was deserted; his very boots were gone; and the craven heart leapt, for all its resolution.

Moya returned to the verandah in time to see the new chum, Ives, coming at a canter through the pines. She cut him off at the barracks, where, however, he flung himself from the saddle and almost into her arms.

"I beg your pardon, Miss Bethune! Forgotten something as usual, you see!"

Hurry and worry were behind his smile. Yet Moya had the heart to detain him.

"Good morning, Mr. Ives. Where's everybody?"

"Gone mustering."

"Not my brother?"

"No; he's gone with the police."

"The police."

"You know, they've gone to follow up some tracks—"

"Oh, yes, I know!" cried Moya.

So Theodore was hand-in-glove with the enemy! Not that the police were the enemy at all; they were only his enemies; but the fact remained that Theodore was one of them. Very likely he had already made them a present of his suspicions; nothing likelier, or more fitting, than the exposure of her "lover" through her own brother's agency. It will be seen that her bitterness against one was rapidly embittering Moya's view of all and sundry. She was not original in that.

"I forgot my water-bag," the jackeroo remarked. "I shall have to gallop to catch them up."

But he was too polite to move.

"Must you catch them up?" inquired Moya, in flattering dumps: but indeed it would be deadly at the station all day, and such a day, without a soul to speak to!

"Well, they won't wait for me, because they told me what to do," said Ives on reflection.

"And what have you to do?" asked Moya, smiling.

"Go down the fence; it's easiest, you know."

•

"But what are you all going to do? What does this mustering mean?"

Ives determined in his own mind to blow the odds. He was not only a gentleman; he was a young man; and Miss Bethune should have all the information she wanted and he could give. Ives began to appreciate her attractions, and Rigden's good fortune, for the first time as they deserved. It would be another place after the marriage. She was a ripper when you got her to yourself.

Aloud he explained the mustering as though he had the morning to spare. It meant sweeping up all the sheep in a given paddock, either to count them out, or to shift them altogether if feed or water was failing where they were. A big job in any case, but especially so in Big Bushy, which was by far the largest paddock on Eureka; it was seven miles by seven.

"And do you generally go mustering at a night's notice?"

"No, as a rule we know about it for days before; but last night the boss—I beg your pardon—"

"What for?" said Moya. "I like to hear him called that."

And she would have liked it, she hardly knew why. But he was not her boss, and never would be.

"Thanks awfully. Well, then, the boss found a tank lower than he expected in Butcher-boy, that's the killing-sheep paddock, and it's next door to Big Bushy, which is stocked with our very best. If the tanks were low in Butcher-boy, they might be lower still in Big Bushy—"

"Why?" asked Moya, like a good Bethune.

"Oh, I don't know; only the boss seemed to think so; and of course it wouldn't do to let our best sheep bog. So we've got to shift every hoof into Westwells, where there's the best water on the run."

Moya said no more. This seemed genuine. Only she was suspicious now of every move of Rigden's; she could not help it.

"And why must you have a water-bag?" she asked, for asking's sake.

"Oh, we never go without one in this heat. The boss won't let us. So of course I went and forgot mine. I'm no good in the bush, Miss Bethune!"

"Not even at mustering?" asked sympathetic Moya.

"Why, Miss Bethune, that's the hardest thing of the lot, and it's where I'm least use. It's my sight," said the young fellow ruefully; "I'm as blind as a mole. You ought to be able to see sheep at three miles, but I can't swear to them at three hundred yards."

"That's a drawback," said Moya, looking thoughtfully at the lad.

"It is," sighed he. "Then I haven't a dog, when I do see 'em; altogether it's no sinecure for me, though they do give me the fence; and—and I'm afraid I really ought to be making a start, Miss Bethune."

The outward eye of Moya was still fixed upon him, but what it really saw was herself upon that lonely verandah all day long—waiting for the next nice development—and waiting alone.

"I have excellent eyes," she observed at length.

"To say the least!" cried her cavalier.

"I meant for practical purposes," rejoined Moya, with severity. "I'm sure that I could see sheep at three miles."

"I shouldn't wonder," said he enviously.

"And I see you have a spare horse in the yard."

"Yes, in case of accidents."

"And I know you have a lady's saddle."

"It was got for you."

Moya winced, but her desire was undiminished.

"I mean to be the accident, Mr. Ives," said she.

"And come mustering?" he cried. "And be my—my—"

"The very eyes of you," said Moya, nodding. "I shall be ready in three minutes!"

And she left him staring, and bereft of breath, but flushed as much with pleasure as with the rosy glow of the Riverina sunrise which fell upon him even as she spoke; she was on the verandah before he recovered his self-possession.

"Your horse'll be ready in two!" he bawled, and rushed to make good his word. Moya had to remind him of the water-bag after all.

First and last she had not delayed him so very long, and the red blob of a sun was but clear of the horizon when they obtained their first unimpeded view of it. This was when they looked back from the gate leading into Butcher-boy: the homestead pines still ran deep into the red, and an ink-pot would still have yielded their hue.

In Butcher-boy, which was three miles across, there was nothing for them to do but to ride after their shadows and to talk as they rode, neck and neck, along the fluted yellow ribbon miscalled a road, between tufts of sea-green saltbush and faraway clumps of trees.

"I wish I wasn't such a duffer in the bush," said Ives, resolved to make the most of the first lady he had met for months. "The rum thing is that I'm frightfully keen on the life."

"Are you really?" queried Moya, and she was interested on her own account, for what might have been.

"Honestly," said Ives, "though I begin to see it isn't the life for me. The whole thing appeals to one, somehow; getting up in the middle of the night (though it was an awful bore), running up the horses (though I can't even crack a stock-whip), and just now the station trees against the sunrise. It's so open and fresh and free, and unlike everything else; it gets at me to the core; but, of course, they don't give me my rations for that."

"Should you really like to spend all your days here?"

"No; but I shouldn't be surprised if I were to spend half my nights here for the term of my natural life! I shall come back to these paddocks in my dreams. I can't tell why, but I feel it in my bones; it's the light, the smell, the extraordinary sense of space, and all the little things as well. The dust and scuttle of the sheep when two or three are gathered together; it's really beastly, but I shall smell it and hear it till I die."

Moya glanced sidelong at her companion, and all was enthusiasm behind the dusty spectacles. There was something in this new chum after all. Moya wondered what.

"You're not going to stick to it, then?"

Ives laughed.

"I'm afraid it won't stick to me. I can't see sheep, I'm no real good with horses, and I couldn't even keep the station books; the owner said my education had been sadly neglected (one for Rugby, that was!) when he was up here the other day. It's only through Mr. Rigden's good-nature that I'm hanging on, and because—I—can't—tear myself away."

"And what do you think of doing eventually?"

"Oh, I don't know. I shall go home again, I suppose; I only came out for the voyage. After that, goodness knows; I was no real use at school either."

Insensibly the rocking-chair canter of the bush horses had lapsed into the equally easy amble which is well-nigh their one alternative; and the shadows were shortening, and the back of the neck and the ears were beginning to burn. The jackeroo was sweeping the horizon for pure inexplicable delight in its dirty greens and yellows; but had quite forgotten that he ought already to have been scouring it for sheep.

"And so the boss is good-natured, is he?" said Moya, she could not have told herself why; for she would not have admitted that it could afford her any further satisfaction to hear his praises.

"Good-natured?" cried the jackeroo. "He's all that and much more; there's not a grander or a straighter chap in Riverina, and we all swear by him; but—well, he is the boss, and let's you know it."

A masterful man; and Moya had wanted her master all these years! She asked no more questions, and they rode a space in silence, Ives glancing sidelong in his turn, and in his heart congratulating Rigden more and more.

"By Jove," he cried at last, "I think I shall have to get you to use your influence on my behalf!"

"For what?" asked Moya, wincing again.

"Another chance! They mustn't give me the sack just yet—I must be here when you come. It's the one thing we need—a lady. It's the one thing he needs to make him as nearly perfect as it's comfortable for other people for a man to be. And I simply must be here to see."

"Let's canter," said Moya. The blood came rushing to his face.

"I apologise," he cried. "It was horrid cheek of me, I know!"

Moya's reassuring smile was all kindly, and not all forced; indeed, the tears were very close to the surface, and she could not trust herself to say much.

"Not cheek at all," was what she did say, with vigour. "Only—you'll change your mind."

With that her eyes glistened for an instant; and young Ives loved her himself. But neither of them was sorry when another gate grew large above the horses' ears, with posts and wires dwindling into perspective on either side to mark the eastern frontier of Big Bushy.

CHAPTER VIII

THE KIND OF LIFE

"Now what do we do, Mr. Ives?"

He had shut the gate and joined her on a sandy eminence, whence Moya was seeking to prove the excellence of her eyesight at the very outset. But the paddock had not got its name for nothing; it was overrun with the sombre scrub, short and thick as lichen on a rock; and from the open spaces no sheep swam into Moya's ken.

"Turn sharp to the left, and follow the fence," replied the jackeroo.

"But I can't see a solitary sheep!"

"No, because you're looking slap into the paddock; that's the ground the others are going over, and they've already cleared it as far as we can see for the scrub. Each man takes his own line of country from this gate to the one opposite—seven miles away—and collects every hoof on the way. My line is the left-hand fence. Got to keep it in sight, and drive everything down it, and right round to the gate."

"Well, my line is yours," said Moya, smiling; and they struck off together from the track.

"It's the long way round, but we can't miss it," said Ives; "all we have to do is to hug the fence. Slightly inglorious, but I'd rather that than make a fool of myself in the middle."

"Is it so very difficult to ride straight through the bush?"

"The most difficult thing in the world. Why, only the other week—"

"I see some!"

The girl was pointing with her riding-switch, to make other use of it next instant. Her mount, a shaggy-looking roan mare, as yet imperfectly appreciated by Moya, proved unexpectedly open to persuasion, and found her gallop in a stride. Ives followed, though he could see nothing but sand and saltbush in the direction indicated. Sheep there were, however, and a fair mob of them, whose behaviour was worthy of their kind. In all docility they stood until the last instant, then broke into senseless stampede, with the horses at their stubby tails.

"Round them up," cried Ives, "but look out! That mare can turn in her own length, and will when they do!"

The warning was timely to the very second: almost simultaneously the sheep doubled, and round spun both horses as in the air. Moya jerked and swayed, but kept her seat. Ives headed the mob for the fence, and for the moment the nonsense was out of them.

"Bravo, Miss Bethune!" said he. "You'll make a better bushman than ever I should."

Moya clouded like an April sky; the instant before she had been deliciously flushed and excited. Her companion, however, was happily intent upon his sheep.

"That's the way to start," he said, "with fifty or sixty at one swoop; you can work a mob like that; it's the five or six that give the trouble. I have reason to know! There's a corner of one of the paddocks in our South Block where a few of the duffers have a meet every morning, just because there's some water they can smell across the fence; won't draw to their own water at the opposite corner of their own paddock, not they! No, there they'd stick and die of thirst if one of us wasn't sent to rout them out. It was my billet every day last week, and a tougher one I never want. One time there was less than half a dozen of 'em: think of driving five weak sheep through eight or nine miles of scrub without a dog! It would be ten miles if I followed both fences religiously; but I'm getting so that I can cut off a pretty fair corner. Yes, it's pretty hard graft, as they say up here, a day like that; but your water-bag holds nectar, while it lasts; and may your wedding-cake taste as good as the bit of browny under a pine, Miss Bethune!"

"What's browny?" asked Moya hastily.

"Raisins and baking-powder," said Ives, with a laugh; "but I've got enough for two in my pocket, so you shall sample it whenever you like. By the way, aren't you thirsty yet?"

Moya was.

"It's the dust from the sheep, which you profess to relish, Mr. Ives."

"Only because it's like no other dust," explained the connoisseur. "And water-bag water's like no other kind."

The canvas bag was wet and heavy as he detached it from the saddle and handed it to Moya after drawing the cork from the glass mouthpiece; and from the latter Moya drank as to the manner born, the moist bag shrinking visibly between her hands.

"Steady!" cried Ives, "or we shall perish of thirst before we strike the gate. Well, what do you think of it?"

"A little canvassy, but I never tasted anything cooler, or more delicious," said Moya in all sincerity, for already the sun was high, and the dry heat of it stupendous.

The jackeroo sighed as he replaced the cork after a very modest sip.

"Ah!" said he, "I wish we were taking sheep to water in the paddock I was telling you about! Long before you get to their water, you strike a covered-in tank, that is if you cut off your corner properly and hit the other fence in the right place. It's really more like a well, without much water in it, but with a rope and a bucket with a hole in it. That bucket's the thing! You fill it a bumper, but it runs out faster than it comes up, and you're lucky if you can pour a wineglassful into the crown of your hat; but that wineglassful's sweeter than the last drop from the bag; it's sweeter than honey from the honeycomb, and I shall say so all my life!"

The boy's enthusiasm was very hard on Moya. It pricked every impression deep in her heart for ever; she caught the contagion of his acute receptivity, upon which the veriest trifles stamped themselves with indelible definition; and it was the same with her. She felt that she should never quite lose the sharp sensations of this one day of real bush life, her first and her last.

Down the fence they fell in with frequent stragglers, and the mob absorbed them in its sweep; then Moya made a sortie to the right, and Ives lost sight of her through the cloud of dust in which she rode, till the beat of hoofs came back with a scuttle of trotters, and the mob was swollen by a score at least, and the thickening cloud pierced by Moya radiant with success. Her habit was powdered as with sullen gold, and the brown gold streamed in strands from her adorable head. Ives worshipped her across the yellow gulf between their horses.

"Where's the dog?" she asked. "I'm certain that I heard one barking."

He turned his head and she heard it again, while the lagging rearguard broke into a run.

"Yet you say you are no bushman!" remonstrated Moya. "No wonder you can do without a four-wheeled dog!"

"It's my one worthy accomplishment," said the barker, modestly; "picked it up in that other paddock; simply dumb with it, sometimes, when I strike the covered-in well I was telling you about. But here we are at the corner; there's a seven-mile fence to travel now, and then as much again as we've done already. Sure you can stand it, Miss Bethune?"

"Is there any water on the way, if we run short?" queried Moya.

Ives considered.

"Well, there's an abandoned whim in the far corner, at the end of this fence; the hut's a ruin, but the four-hundred-gallon tank belonging to it was left good for the sake of anybody who might turn up thirsty. Of course it may be empty, but we'll see."

"We'll chance it, Mr. Ives, and have another drink now!"

For it was nearing noon, and beyond the reek of the travelling mob, now some couple of hundred strong, the lower air quivered as though molten metal lay cooling in the sand. Moya had long since peeled off her riding gloves, and already the backs of her hands were dreadfully inflamed. But the day would be her first and last in the real bush; she would see it through. She never felt inclined to turn back but once, and that was when a sheep fell gasping by the way, its eyes glazed and the rattle in its neck. Moya insisted on the remnant of water being poured down its throat and the tears were on her cheeks when they rounded up the mob once more, leaving a carcass behind them after all, and the blue crows settling on the fence.

Otherwise the seven miles were uneventful travelling; for even Moya's eyes discerned few more sheep on their side of the wires; and beyond these, to the left, was the long and ragged edge of a forest so dense (though low) that Moya, riding with Ives at the tail of the mob, said it was no wonder there were no sheep at all on the other side.

"Oh, but that's not Eureka over there," explained Ives; "that's the worst bit of country in the whole of Riverina. No one will take it up; it's simply fenced in by the fences of the blocks all round."

Moya asked what it was called. The name seemed familiar to her. It was Blind Man's Block.

"Ah! I know," she said presently, suppressing a sigh. "I heard them speaking of it on the verandah last night."

"Yes, Spicer was advising your brother to sample it if he wanted an adventure; but don't you let him, Miss Bethune. I wouldn't lose sight of the fence in Blind Man's Block for all I'm ever likely to be worth: there was a man's skeleton found there just before I came, and goodness knows how many there are that never will be found. Aha! there's the whim at last. I'm jolly glad!"

"So am I," said Moya, with a little shudder; and she fixed her eyes upon some bold black timbers that cut the sky like a scaffold a mile or two ahead; yet more than once her eyes returned to the line of dingy scrub across the fence to the left, as if fascinated by its sinister repute.

"We must bustle them along, by Jove!" exclaimed Ives, and he yelped and barked with immediate effect. "You can't do more than a couple of miles an hour with sheep; and at that rate we shan't be at the gate much before three o'clock; for I see that it's already close upon one."

"But how do you see it?" asked Moya curiously. "I've never seen you look at a watch."

Ives smiled, for he had led up to the question, and was about to show off in yet another branch of the bushman's craft which even he had succeeded in mastering.

"The fences are my watch," said he; "they happen to run due east and west and north and south on this station. This one is north and south. So at noon the shadows of the posts lie exactly under the wires: put your head between 'em, and when the bottom wire bisects the shadow it's as near noon as you would make it with a quadrant and sextant. The rest comes by practice. Another dodge is to put a stick plumb in the ground and watch when the shadow is shortest; that's your meridian."

"Yet you say you are no good in the bush!"

"I have two of the unnecessary qualifications, Miss Bethune, and I've taken care to let you see them both," laughed the open youth. "My only other merit as a bushman is a good rule which I am sorry to say I've broken through talking to you. I always have my lunch at twelve under the biggest tree in sight. And I think we shall find something in that pine-ridge within a cooee on the right."

But they could not find shade for two, and Moya voted the pine-tree a poor parasol; whereupon her companion showed off still further by squatting under the very girths of his horse, but once more spoilt his own effect by confessing that they gave him the quietest horse on the station. So the two of them divided bread and meat and "browny" for one, of which last Moya expressed approval; but not until she was asked; for she was not herself during this interval of inaction, or rather she was herself once more. Care indeed had ridden behind her all the morning; but now the black imp was back before her troubled eyes, and for the moment they saw nothing else. But Ives began to see and to wonder what in the world it could be. She was engaged to one of the best of good fellows. She took to the bush as to her proper element, and but now had seemed enchanted with her foretaste of the life. Why then the grim contour of so sweet a face, the indignant defiance in the brooding eyes? Ives thought and thought until his youthful egoism assumed the blame, and shot him from his precarious shelter, all anxiety and remorse.

"What a brute I am! You're simply perishing of thirst!"

Moya coloured, but had the wit to accept his construction.

"Well, it isn't your fault, at any rate, Mr. Ives."

"But I might have ridden on and filled the bag; there's certain to be something in the tank at the hut."

"Then let's ride on together."

"No, you ride ahead and fill the water-bag. It'll save time, Miss Bethune, because I can be cutting off the corner with the mob."

But the mob had first to be rounded up, for it had split and scattered, and over a square mile every inch of shade was covered by a crouching fleece. The mounted Ives made a circuit with his patent yelp, and each tuft and bush shook out its pure merino. It was harder work to head them off the fence at an angle of forty-five, and to aim for the other fence before a post of it was discernible by near-sighted eyes. Ives was too busy to follow Moya's excursion, but was not less delighted than amazed at the speed with which she returned from the hut.

"Good riding, Miss Bethune! A drink, a drink, my kingdom—"

Moya's face stopped him.

"I'm sorry to say I've got nothing for you to drink, Mr. Ives."

Ives licked the roof of his mouth, but tried to be heroic.

"Well, have you had some yourself?"

"No. I—the fact is I couldn't see the tank."

"Not see the tank! Why, you ought to be able to see it from here; no, it's on the other side; give me the bag!"

"What for?" asked Moya, more startled than he saw.

"I'll go this time. You stay with the sheep."

"But what's the good of going if the tank has been removed? If I couldn't see it I'm sure you can't," said Moya bluntly.

"Did you ride right up?"

"Of course I did."

And Moya smiled.

"Well, at all events there's the whim-water. It's rather brackish—"

"Thank you," said Moya, smiling still.

"But I thought you were knocked up with thirst? I am, I can tell you. And it's only rather salt—that's why we've given up using that whim—but it's not salt enough to make you dotty!"

Moya maintained the kindly demeanour which she had put on with her smile; it cost her an effort, however.

"Go on your own account, by all means," said she; "but not on mine, for I shan't touch a drop. I'm really not so thirsty as you suppose; let me set you an example of endurance, Mr. Ives!"

That was enough for him. He was spurring and yelping round his mob next moment. But Moya did not watch him; she had turned in her saddle to take a last look at the black hieroglyph of a whim, with the little iron roof blazing beside it in the sun. She even shaded her eyes with one sunburnt hand, as if to assure herself that she had made no mistake.

"So the whim is abandoned, and the hut unoccupied?"

"Yes, ever since Mr. Rigden has been manager. I hear it was one of his first improvements."

They had struck the farther fence, and the mob was well in hand along the wires. Moya and the jackeroo were ambling leisurely behind, and nothing could have been more natural than Moya's questions.

"And the hut is unoccupied?" was her next.

"Quite; as a matter of fact, it's unfit for occupation."

"Yet you wanted me to drink the water!"

"That might have been all right; besides any water's better than none when you're as thirsty as I thought you were."

Moya said no more about her thirst; it was intolerable; but they must be getting near the gate at last. She was silent for a time, a time of imaginative torment, for her mind ran on the latter end of such sufferings as she was only beginning to endure. She was just uncomfortable enough to have a dreadful inkling of the stages between discomfort and death.

"It's a pity not to use the hut," she said at length.

"I believe it was more bother than the class of water was worth," returned Ives. "Yes, now I think of it, I remember hearing that they couldn't get men to stay there. Blind Man's Block used to give them the creeps. They're frightfully superstitious, these back-blockers!"

"I'm not surprised," said Moya, with a shudder. "I never want to see Blind Man's Block again, or the hut either."

"But you will, you know!" the jackeroo reminded her. And that put an end to the conversation.

Over a thousand sheep were at the gate waiting for them, with half a dozen horses and as many men. Of course Ives was the last to arrive with his mob, but the goodly numbers of the latter combined with the amazing apparition of Moya to save her friend from the reprimand he seldom failed to earn. Rigden came galloping to meet them, and for both men's sake Moya treated him prettily enough in front of Ives. Even through that day's coat of red, Rigden glowed, and told Ives that he should make something of him yet. His water-bag was not quite empty, and Moya had enough to make her long for more as she cantered with the bag to Ives, who had forged discreetly ahead.

"Don't let him know we went so long without, Mr. Ives!"

And his cracked lips were sealed upon the subject.

"Of course you cut off the corner, and didn't go right round by the hut?" said Rigden, riding up; and the jackeroo felt justified in speaking strictly for himself; and thought it so like Miss Bethune not to compromise him by saying how near to the hut they had been: for Moya said nothing at all.

"And now you shall see a count-out," cried Rigden, in better spirits than ever, "as soon as we've boxed the mobs."

"Boxed them!" cried Moya. "Where?"

"Joined them, I mean. To think of your coming mustering of your own accord, Moya!"

His voice had fallen; she did not lower hers.

"It's one of the most interesting days I ever had," she informed all within hearing; "now let me see the end of it, and I'll go back happy."

The adjective was not convincing, but Rigden would not let it dishearten him. The very fact of her presence was the end of his despair.

"I met one of our rabbiters, and arranged for tea at his tent," he said. "He little expects a lady, but you'll have to come."

The prospect had material attractions which Moya was much too honest to deny. "Then make haste and count!" was what she said.

And that followed which appealed to Moya more than all that had gone before. The gate gaped wide, and Rigden on foot put his back to one post. The rest kept their saddles, and began gently rounding up the mob, till it formed a pear-shaped island of consolidated wool, with the headland stretching almost to Rigden's feet. He turned and beckoned to the jackeroo.

"Tally, Ives!"

"Tally, sir," the jackeroo rejoined, and urged his horse to the front. He had managed to drift back to Moya's side, to ensure her complete appreciation of a manoeuvre he delighted in, but at the word of command he was gone without a glance, and visible responsibility settled on his rigid shoulders.

Real dogs kept the mob together, but the head stood stubborn at the gate, with none to lead the way till Rigden touched the foremost fleece with his toe and the race began. Slowly and singly at the start, as the first grains slip through the hour-glass; by wondering twos and threes, as the reluctant leaders were seen alive and well in the farther paddock; thereafter by the dozen abreast, so far as the ordinary eye could judge; but Rigden was the only one that knew, as he stood in the gateway, beating time to the stampede with raised forefinger, and nodding it with bent head.

"Hundred!" he called after the first half-minute, and "hundred!" in quarter of a minute more, while Ives raised a hand each time and played five-finger exercises with the other hand upon his thigh. At the same time Rigden vanished in a yellow cloud, whence his voice came quicker and thicker, crying hundred after hundred above the dull din of a scuffling and scuttling as of a myriad mice heard through a microphone. And the dusty fleeces disappeared on one side of the cloud to reappear on the other until all were through.

"And seventy-two!" concluded Rigden hoarsely. "How many, Ives?"

"Two thousand one hundred and seventy-two," replied the jackeroo promptly.

"Sure?"

"Certain, sir."

"And so am I," said Moya, riding forward, "for I kept tally too. Yes, the hundreds are all right; but nothing will convince me that they were hundreds; you might as well count the falling drops in a shower!"

Rigden smiled as he wiped the yellow deposit from his scarlet face.

"I may be one per cent. out," said he; "but if I'm more I deserve the sack."

So Moya allowed that it was the most marvellous performance her own eyes had ever seen; and these were full of an unconscious admiration for Rigden and his prowess; but Rigden was conscious of it, and his chin lifted, and his jaw set, and his burnt face glowed again.

Two of the musterers were told off to take the sheep to their new tank, for their own dust had set them bleating for a drink; the rest lit their pipes and turned their horses' heads for home; but Ives was instructed to stop at the rabbiter's camp and tell him whom to expect.

"It would be unfair to spring you on the poor chap," said Rigden to Moya.

Ives also had a last word to say to her, though he had to say it before the boss.

"That was something to see, wasn't it, Miss Bethune? Doesn't it make you keener than ever on the bush? Or isn't that possible?"

And he took off his wideawake as he shot ahead; but Rigden and Moya rode on together without speaking.

CHAPTER IX

PAX IN BELLO

In happier circumstances the rabbiter's camp would have had less charm for Moya. Its strings of rabbit-skins would have offended two senses, and she would have objected openly to its nondescript dogs. The tent among the trees would never have struck Moya as a covetable asylum, while the rabbiter himself, on his haunches over the fire, could not have failed to impress her as a horrid old man and nothing else. He was certainly very ragged, and dirty, and hot; and he never said "sir," or "miss," or "glad to see you." Yet he could cook a chop to the fraction of a turn; and Moya could eat it off his own tin platter, and drink tea by the pint out of a battered pannikin, with no milk in it, but more brown sugar than enough. The tea, indeed, she went so far as to commend in perfectly sincere superlatives.

"Oh, the tea's not so dusty," said the rabbiter grimly; "it didn't ought to be at the price you charge for it in your store, mister! But the tea don't matter so much; it's the water's the thing; and what's the matter with the water in these here tanks, that you should go shifting all your sheep, Mr. Rigden?"

This was obviously Rigden's business, and Moya, pricking an involuntary ear, thought that he might have said so in as many words. But Rigden knew his type, and precisely when and in what measure to ignore its good-humoured effrontery.

"It's the sort of thing to do in time, or not at all," said he. "You catch me wait till my sheep begin to bog!"

"Bog!" cried the rabbiter. "Who said they were beginning to bog? I tell you there's tons of good water in this here tank; you come and look!"

And he made as if to lead the way to the long yellow lip of excavation that showed through the clump. But Rigden shook his head and smiled, under two scrutinies; and this time he did not say that he knew his own business best; but his manner betrayed no annoyance.

Moya, however, contrived to obtain a glimpse of the water as they rode away. It looked cool and plentiful in the slanting sunlight—a rippling parallelogram flecked with gold. There was very little mud about the margin.

"So it is quite an event, this mustering?"

The question had been carefully considered over a mile or so of lengthening shadows, with the cool hand of evening on their brows already. It was intended to lead up to another question, which, however, Rigden's reply was so fortunate as to defer.

"Oh, it's nothing to some of our other functions," said he.

And Moya experienced such a twinge of jealousy that she was compelled to ask what those functions were; otherwise she would never know.

"First and foremost there's the shearing; if this interests you, I wonder what you'll think of that?" speculated Rigden, exactly as though they had no quarrel. "It's the thing to see," he continued, with deliberate enthusiasm: "it means mustering the whole run, that does, and travelling mob after mob to the shed; and then the drafting; that's another thing for you to see, though it's nothing to the scene in the shed. But it's no good telling you about that till you've seen the shed itself. We shore thirty-eight thousand last year. I was over the board myself. Two dozen shearers and a round dozen rouseabouts—"

"I'm afraid it's Greek to me," interrupted Moya dryly; but she wished it was not.

"—and no swearing allowed in the shed; half-a-crown fine each time; that very old ruffian who gave us tea just now said it was a lapsus lingua when I fined him! You never know what they've been, not even the roughest of them. But to come back to the shed: no smoking except at given times when they all knock off for quarter-of-an-hour, and the cook's boy comes down the board with pannikins of tea and shearers' buns. Oh, they take good care of themselves, these chaps, I can tell you; give their cook half-a-crown a week per head, and see he earns it. Then there's a couple of wool-pressers, a wool-sorter from Geelong, Ives branding the bales, Spicer seeing the drays loaded and keeping general tally, and the boss of the shed with his eye on everything and everybody. Oh, yes, a great sight for you—your first shearing!"

Moya shook her head without speaking, but Rigden was silenced at last. He had rattled on and on with the hope of reawakening her enthusiasm first, then her sympathy, then—but no! He could not keep it up unaided; he must have some encouragement, and she gave him none. He relapsed into silence, but presently proposed a canter. And this brought Moya to her point at last.

"Cantering won't help us," she cried; "do let's be frank! It's partly my fault for beating about the bush; it set you off talking against time, and you know it. But we aren't anywhere near the station yet, and there's one thing you are going to tell me before we get there. Why did you move those sheep?"

Rigden was taken aback.

"You heard me tell that rabbiter," he replied at length.

"But not the truth," said Moya bluntly. "You know you don't usually have these musters at a moment's notice; you know there was no occasion for one to-day. Do let us have the truth in this one instance— that—that I may think a little better of you, Pelham!"

It was the first time that she had called him by any name since the very beginning of their quarrel. And her voice had softened. And for one instant her hand stretched across and lay upon his arm.

"Very well!" he said brusquely. "It was to cover up some tracks."

"Thank you," said Moya; and her tone surprised him, it was so free from irony, so earnest, so convincing in its simple sincerity.

"Why do you thank me?" he asked suspiciously.

"I like to be trusted," she said. "And I like to be told the truth."

"If only you would trust me!" he cried from his heart. "From the first I have told you all I could, and only asked you to believe that I was acting for the best in all the rest. That I can say: according to my lights I am still acting for the best. I may have done wrong legally, but morally I have not. I have simply sheltered and shielded a fellow creature who has already suffered out of all proportion to his fault; but I admit that I have done the thing thoroughly. Yes, I'll be frank with you there. I gave him a start last night on my own horse, as indeed you know. I laid a false scent first; then I arranged this muster simply and solely to destroy the real scent. I don't know that it was necessary; but I do know that neither the police nor anybody else will ever get on his tracks in Big Bushy; there has been too much stock over the same ground since."

There was a grim sort of triumph in his tone, which Moya came near to sharing in her heart. She felt that she could and would share it, if only he would tell her all.

"Why keep him in Big Bushy?" she quietly inquired.

"Keep him there?" reiterated Rigden. "Who's doing so, Moya?"

"I don't know; but he was there this morning."

"This morning?"

"Yes, in the hut. I saw him."

"You saw him in the hut? The fool!" cried Rigden. "So he let you see him! Did you speak to him?"

"No, thank you," said Moya, with unaffected disgust. "I was riding up to see whether there was any water at the hut. I turned my horse straight round, and did without."

"And didn't Ives see him?"

"No, he was with the sheep; when I joined him and said I could see no tank, which was perfectly true, he wanted to go back for the water himself."

She stopped abruptly.

"Well?"

"I wouldn't let him," said Moya. "That's all."

She rode on without glancing on either hand. Dusk had fallen; there were no more shadows. The sun had set behind them; but Moya still felt the glow she could not see; and it was in like manner that she was aware also of Rigden's long gaze.

"The second time," he said softly at last.

"The second time what?"

This tone was sharp.

"That you've come to my rescue, Moya."

"That I've descended to your level, you mean!"

He caught her rein angrily.

"You've no right to say that without knowing!"

"Whose fault is it that I don't know?"

He loosed her rein and caught her hand instead, and held it against all resistance. Yet Moya did not resist. He hurt her, and she welcomed the pain.

"Moya, I would tell you this moment if I thought it would be for your good and mine. It wouldn't—so why should I? It is something that you would never, never forgive!"

"You mean the secret of the man's hold upon you?"

"Yes," he said, after a pause.

"You are wrong," said Moya, quickly. "It shows how little you know me! I could forgive anything—anything—that is past and over. Anything but your refusal to trust me ... when as you say yourself ... I have twice over...."

She was shaking in her saddle, in a fit of suppressed sobbing the more violent for its very silence. In the deep gloaming it might have been an ague that had seized her; but some tears fell upon his hand holding hers; and next moment that arm was round her waist. Luckily the horses were tired out. And so for a little her head lay on his shoulder as though there were no space between, the while he whispered in her ear with all the eloquence he possessed, and all the passion she desired.

In this she must trust him, else indeed let her never trust him with her life! But she would—she would? Surely one secret withheld was not to part them for all time! And she loved the place after all, he could see that she loved it, nor did she deny it when he paused; she would love the life, he saw that too, and again there was no denial. They had been so happy yesterday! They could be so happy all their lives! But for that it was not necessary that they should tell each other everything. It was not as if he was going to question her right to have and to keep secrets of her own. She was welcome to as many as ever she liked. He happened to know, for example (as a matter of fact, it was notorious), that he was not the first man whom she had fancied she cared about. But did he ask questions about the others? Well, then, she should remember that in his favour. And yet—and yet—she had stood nobly by him in spite of all her feelings! And yes, she had earned the right to know more—to know all—when he remembered that he was risking his liberty and her happiness, and that she had countenanced the risk in her own despite! Ah, if only he were sure of her and her forgiveness; if only he were sure!

"You talk as though you had committed some crime yourself," said Moya; "well, I don't care if you have, so long as you tell me all about it. There is nothing I wouldn't forgive—nothing upon earth—except such secrets from the girl you profess to love."

She had got rid of his arm some time before this, but their hands were still joined in the deepening twilight, until at this he dropped hers suddenly.

"Profess!" he echoed. "Profess, do I? You know better than that, at all events! Upon my soul I've a good mind to tell you after that, and chance the consequences!"

His anger charmed her, as the anger of the right man should charm the right woman. And this time it was she who sought his hand.

"Then tell me now," she whispered. "And you shall see how you have misjudged me."

It was hard on Moya that he was not listening, for she had used no such tone towards him these four-and-twenty hours. And listening he was, but to another sound which reached her also in the pause. It was the thud and jingle of approaching horsemen. Another minute and the white trappings of the mounted police showed through the dusk.

"That you, Mr. Rigden?" said a queer voice for the sergeant. "Can you give us a word, please?"

Rigden had but time to glance at Moya.

"I'll ride on slowly," she said at once; and she rode on the better part of a mile, leaving the way entirely to her good bush steed. At last there was quite a thunder of overtaking hoofs, and Rigden reined up beside her, with the sergeant not far behind. Moya looked round, and the sergeant was without his men, at tactful range.

"Do they guess anything?" whispered Moya.

"Not they!"

"Sure the others haven't gone on to scour Big Bushy?"

"No, only to cross it on their way back. They've given it up, Moya! The sergeant's just coming back for dinner."

His tone had been more triumphant before his triumph was certain, but Moya did not notice this.

"I'm so glad," she whispered, half mischievously, and caught his hand under cloud of early night.

"Are you?" said Rigden, wistfully. "Then I suppose you'll say you're glad about something else. You won't be when the time comes! But now it's all over you shall have your way, Moya; come for a stroll after dinner, and I'll tell you—every—single—thing!"

CHAPTER X

THE TRUTH BY INCHES

He told her with his back against the gate leading into Butcher-boy. Moya heard him and stood still. Behind her rose the station pines, and through the pines peeped hut and house, in shadow below, but with each particular roof like a clean tablecloth in the glare of the risen moon. A high light or so showed in the verandah underneath; this was Bethune's shirt-front, that the sergeant's breeches, and those transitory red-hot pin-heads their cigars. Rigden had superb sight. He could see all this at something like a furlong's range. Yet all that he did see was Moya with the moon upon her, a feathery and white silhouette, edged with a greater whiteness, and crowned as with gold.

"Your father!"

"Yes, I am his son and heir."

Her tone was low with grief and horror, but his was unintentionally sardonic. It jarred upon the woman, and reacted against the man. Moya's first feeling had been undefiled by self; but in an instant her tears were poisoned at their fount.

"And you told me your father was dead!"

The new note was one of the eternal scale between man and woman. It was the note of unbridled reproach.

"Never in so many words, I think," said Rigden, unfortunately.

"In so many words!" echoed Moya, but the sneer was her last. "I hate such contemptible distinctions!" she cried out honestly. "Better have cheated me wholesale, as you did the police; there was something thorough about that."

"And I hope that you can now see some excuse for it," rejoined Rigden with more point.

"For that, yes!" cried Moya at once. "Oh, dear, yes, no one can blame you for screening your poor father. I forgive you for cheating the police—it would have been unnatural not to—but I never, never shall forgive you for what was unnatural—cheating me."

Rigden took a sharper tone.

"You are too fond of that word," said he, "and I object to it as between me and you."

"You have earned it, though!"

"I deny it. I simply held my tongue about a tragedy in my own family which you could gain nothing by knowing. There was no cheating in that."

"I disagree with you!" said Moya very hotly, but he went on as though she had not spoken.

"You speak as though I had hushed up something in my own life. Can't you see the difference? He was convicted under another name; it was a thing nobody knew but ourselves; nobody need ever have known. Or so I thought," he ended in a wretched voice.

But Moya was outwardly unmoved.

"All the more reason why you should have told me, and trusted me," she insisted.

"God knows I thought of it! But I knew the difference it would make. And I was right!"

It was his turn to be bitter, and Moya's to regain complete control.

"So you think it's that that makes the difference now?"

"Of course it is."

"Would you believe me if I assured you it was not?"

"No; you might think so; but I know."

"You know singularly little about women," said Moya after a pause.

And her tone shook him. But he said that he could only judge by the way she had taken it now.

There was another pause, in which the proud girl wrestled with her pride. But at last she told him he was very dull. And she drew a little nearer, with the ghost of other looks behind her tears.

But the high moon just missed her face.

And Rigden was very dull indeed.

"You had better tell me everything, and give me a chance," she said dryly.

"What's the use, when the mere fact is enough?"

"I never said it was."

"Oh, Moya, but you know it must be. Think of your people!"

"Why should I?"

"They will have to know."

"I don't see it."

"Ah, but they will," said Rigden, with dire conviction. And though the change in Moya was now apparent even to him, it wrought no answering change in Rigden; on the contrary, he fell into a brown study, with dull eyes fixed no longer upon Moya, but on the high lights in the verandah far away.

"There's so little to tell," he said at length. "It was a runaway match, and a desperately bad bargain for my dear mother, yet by no means the unhappy marriage you would suppose. I have that from her own dear lips, and I don't think it so extraordinary as I did once. A bad man may still be the one man for a good woman, and make her happier than the best of good fellows; it was so in their case. My father was and is a bad man; there's no mincing the matter. I've stood by him for what he is to me, not for what he is in himself, for he has gone from bad to worse, like most prisoners. He was in trouble when he married my mother; the police were on his tracks even then: they came out here under a false name."

"And your name?" asked Moya, pertinently yet not unkindly; indeed she was standing close beside him now.

"That is not false," said Rigden. "My mother used it from the time of her trouble. She would not bring me up under an alias; but she took care not to let his people or hers get wind of her existence; never wrote them a line in her poorest days, though her people would have taken her back—without him. That wouldn't do for my mother. Yet nothing else was possible. He was sent to the hulks for life."

Moya's face, turned to the light at last, was shining like the moon itself; and the tears in her eyes were tears of enthusiasm, almost of pride.

"It was fine of her!" she said, and caught his hand.

"She was fine," he answered simply. Yet Moya's hand had no effect. He looked at it wistfully, but let it go without an answering clasp. And the girl's pride bled again.

She hardly heard his story after that. Yet it was a story to hear. The villain had not been a villain of the meaner dye, but one of parts, courage among them.

"There have been no bushrangers in your time," said Rigden; "but you may have heard of them?"

"I remember all about the Kellys," said honest Moya. "I'm not so young as all that."

"Did you ever hear of Captain Bovill?"

"I know the name, nothing more."

"I am glad of that," said Rigden, grimly. "It is the name by which my unhappy father is going down to Australian history as one of its most notorious criminals. The gold-fields were the beginning of the end of him, as of many a better man; he could not get enough out of his claim, so he took it from an escort under arms. There was a whole band of them, and they were all taken at last; but it was not the last of Captain Bovill. You have seen the old hulk Success? He was one of the prisoners who seized the launch and killed a warder and a sailor between them; he was one of those sentenced to death and afterwards reprieved. That was in '56; the next year they murdered the Inspector-General; and he was tried for that with fifteen others, but he got off with his neck. He only spoilt his last chance of legal freedom in this life; so he tried to escape again and again; and at last he has succeeded!"

The son's tone was little in keeping with his acts, but the incongruity was very human. There was Moya beside him in the moonlight, but for the last time, whatever she might say or think! And her mind was working visibly.

"Why didn't the police say who it was they were after?" she cried of a sudden; and the blame was back in her voice, for she had found new shoulders for it.

Rigden smiled sadly.

"Don't you see?" he said. "Don't you remember what Harkness said at the start about my fellows harbouring him? But he told me that evening—to think that it was only last night!—as a great secret and a tremendous piece of news. The fact is that my unhappy father was more than notorious in his day; he was popular; and popular sympathy has been the bugbear of the police ever since the Kellys. Not that he has much sympathy for me!" cried Rigden all at once. "Not that I'm acting altogether from a sense of filial duty, however mistaken; no, you shan't run away with any false ideas. It was one for him and two for myself! He had the whip-hand of me, and let me know it; if I gave him away, he'd have given me!"

"If only you had let him! If only you had trusted me," sighed Moya once more. "But you do now, don't you—dear?"

And she touched his coat, for she could not risk the repulse of his hand, though her words went so far—so very far for Moya.

"It's too late now," he said.

But it was incredible! Even now he seemed not to see her hand—hers! Vanity invaded her once more, and her gates stood open to the least and meanest of the besetting host. She make advances to him, to the convict's son! What would her people say? What would Toorak say? What would she not say herself—to herself—of herself—after this nightmare night?

And all because (but certainly for the second time) he had taken no notice of her hand!

When found, however, Moya's voice was as cold as her heart was hot.

"Oh, very well! It is certainly too late if you wish it to be so, and in any case now. But may I ask why you are so keen to save me the trouble of saying so?"

Rigden looked past her towards the station, and there were no more high lights in the verandah; but elsewhere there were voices, and the champing of a bit.

"If you go back now," he said, "you will just be in time to hear."

"Thank you. I prefer to have it here, and from you."

Rigden shrugged his shoulders.

"Then I am no longer a free agent. I am here on parole. I am under arrest."

"Nonsense!"

"I am, though: harbouring the fugitive! They can't put salt on him, so they have on me."

Moya stood looking at him in a long silence, but only hardening as she looked: patience, pity and understanding had gone like so many masts, by the board, and the wreckage in her heart closed it finally against him in the very hour of his more complete disaster.

"And how long have you known this?" she inquired stonily, though the answer was obvious to her mind.

"Ever since we met them on our ride home. They showed me their warrant then. The trooper had done thirty miles for it this afternoon. They wanted to take me straight away. But I persuaded Harkness to come back to dinner and return with me later without fuss."

"Yet you couldn't say one word to me!"

"Not just then. Where was the point? But I arranged with Harkness to tell you now. And by all my gods I've told you everything there is to tell, Moya!"

"You should have told me this first. But you tell nothing till you are forced! I might have known you were keeping the worst up your sleeve! I shouldn't be surprised if the very worst were still to come!"

"It's coming now," said Rigden, bitterly; "it's coming from you, in the most miserable hour of all my existence; you must make it worse! How was I to know the other wouldn't be enough for you? How do I know now?"

"Thank you," said Moya, a knife in her heart, but another in her tongue.

The voices drew nearer through the pines; there was Harkness mounted, with a led horse, and Theodore Bethune on foot. Rigden turned abruptly to the girl.

"There are just two more things to be said. None of them know where he is, and none of them know my motive. You're in both secrets. You'd better keep them—unless you want Toorak to know who it was you were engaged to."

The rest followed without a word. It might have been a scene in a play without words, and indeed the moon chalked the faces of the players, and the Riverina crickets supplied the music with an orchestra some millions strong. The clink of a boot in a stirrup, a thud in the saddle, another clink upon the off side; and Rigden lifting his wideawake as he rode after Harkness through the gate; and Bethune holding the gate open, shutting it after them, and taking Moya's arm as she stood like Lot's wife in the moonlight.

CHAPTER XI

BETHUNE v. BETHUNE

"I don't want to rub things in, or to make things worse," said Theodore, kindly enough, as they approached the house; "but we shall have to talk about them, for all that, Moya."

"I'm ready," was the quick reply. "I'll talk till daylight as long as you won't let me think!"

"That's the right child!" purred her brother. "Come to my room; it's the least bit more remote; and these youths are holding indignation meetings on their own account. Ah! here's one of them."

Spicer had stepped down from the verandah with truculent stride.

"A word with you, Bethune," said he, brusquely.

"Thanks, but I'm engaged to my sister for this dance," replied the airy Theodore. Moya could not stand his tone. Also she heard young Ives turning the horses out for the night, and an inspiration seized her by the heels.

"No, for the next," said she; "I want to speak to Mr. Ives."

And she flew to the horse-yard, where the slip-rails were down, and Ives shooing horse after horse across them like the incurable new chum he was.

"Wait a moment, Mr. Ives. Don't have me trampled to death just yet."

"Miss Bethune!"

And the top rail was up again. But it was not her presence that surprised him. It was her tone.

"A dreadful ending to our day, Mr. Ives!"

"I'm glad to hear you say that," cried the boy, with all his enthusiasm; "to our day, if you like, but that's all! This is the most infernally unjust and high-handed action that ever was taken by the police of any country! Iniquitous—scandalous! But it won't hold water; these squatters are no fools, and every beak in the district's a squatter; they'll see Rigden through, and we'll have him back before any of the hands know a word of what's up."

"But don't they know already?"

"Not they; trust us for that! Why, even Mrs. Duncan has no idea why he's gone. But we shall have him back this time to-morrow, never you fear, Miss Bethune!"

"How far is it to the police-barracks, Mr. Ives?"

"Well, it's fourteen miles to our boundary, and that's not quite half-way."

"Then they won't be there before midnight. Is it the way we went this morning, Mr. Ives?"

"Yes; he's going over the same ground, poor chap, in different company. But he'll come galloping back to-morrow, you take my word for it!"

Ives leant with folded arms upon the restored rail. The animals already turned out hugged the horse-yard fence wistfully. The lucky remnant were licking the last grains of chaff from the bin. Moya drew nearer to the rail.

"Mr. Ives!"

"Miss Bethune?"

"Would you do a favour for me?"

"Would I not!"

"And say nothing about it afterwards?"

"You try me."

"Then leave a horse that I can ride—and saddle—in the yard to-night!"

Ives was embarrassed.

"With pleasure," said he, with nothing of the sort—and began hedging in the same breath. "But—but look here, I say, Miss Bethune! You're never going all that way—"

"Of course I'm not, and if I do it won't be before morning, only first thing then, before the horses are run up. And I don't want you, or anybody, least of all my brother, to come with me, or have the least idea where I've gone, or that I've gone anywhere at all. See? I'm perfectly well able to take care of myself, Mr. Ives. Can I trust you?"

"Of course you can, but—"

"No advice—please—dear Mr. Ives!"

It was Moya at her sweetest, with the moon all over her. She wondered at the time how she forced that smile; but it gained her point.

"Very well," he sighed; "your blood—"

"I shan't lose one drop," said Moya brightly. "And no more questions?"

"Of course not."

"And no tellings?"

"Miss Bethune!"

"Forgive me," said Moya. "I'm more than satisfied. And you're—the—dearest young man in the bush, Mr. Ives!"

The jackeroo swept his wideawake to the earth.

"And you're the greatest girl in the world, though I were to be drawn and quartered for saying so!"

Moya returned to the house with pensive gait. She was not overwhelmed with a present sense of her alleged greatness. On the contrary, she had seldom felt so small and petty. But she could make amends; at least she could try.

Horse-yard and house were not very far apart, but some of the lesser buildings intervened, and Moya had been too full of her own sudden ideas to lend an ear to any or aught but Ives and his replies. So she had missed a word or two which it was just as well for her to miss, and more even than a word. She did notice, however, that Mr. Spicer turned his back as she passed him in the verandah. And she found Theodore dabbing his knuckles in his bedroom.

"What's the matter? What have you done?"

"Oh, nothing."

But tone and look alike betokened some new achievement: they were self-satisfied even for Bethune of the Hall.

"Tell me," demanded Moya.

"Well, if you want to know, I've been teaching one of your back-blockers (yours no more, praises be!) a bit of a lesson. Our friend Spicer. Very offensive to me all day; seemed to think I was inspiring the police. Just now he surpassed himself; wanted me to take off my coat and go behind the pines; in other words to fight."

"And wouldn't you?"

"Not exactly. Take off my coat to him!"

"So what did you do?"

"Knocked him down as I stood."

"You didn't!"

"Very well. Ask Mr. Spicer. I'm sorry for the chap; he meant well; and I admire his pluck."

"What did he do?"

"Got up and went for me bald-headed."

"And you knocked him down again?"

"No," said Theodore, "that time I knocked him out."

And he took a cigarette from his silver case, while Moya regarded him with almost as much admiration as disgust, and more of surprise than of either.

"I didn't know this was one of your accomplishments," said she at length.

"Aha!" puffed Theodore; "nor was it, once upon a time. But there's a certain old prize-fighter at a place called Trumpington, and he taught me the most useful thing I learnt up at Cambridge. The poetic justice of it is that I 'read' with him, so to speak, with a view to these very bush bullies and up-country larrikins. They're too free with their tongues when they're in a good temper, and with their fists when they're not. I suffered from them in early youth, Moya, but I don't fancy I shall suffer any more."

Moya was not so sure. She caught herself matching Theodore and another in her mind, and was not ashamed of the side she took. It made no difference to her own quarrel with the imaginary champion; nothing could or should alter that. But perhaps she had been ungenerous. He seemed to think so. She would show him she was neither ungenerous, nor a coward, before she was done. And after that the deluge.

Hereabouts Moya caught Theodore watching her, a penny for her thoughts in either eye. In an instant she had ceased being disingenuous with herself, and was hating him heartily for having triumphed over an adherent of Rigden, however mistaken; in another she was sharing that adherent's suspicions; in a third, expressing them.

"I shouldn't wonder if Mr. Spicer was quite right!"

"In accusing me of inspiring the police?"

"You suspected the truth last night. Oh, I saw through all that; we won't discuss it. And why should you keep your suspicions to yourself?"

Bethune blew a delicate cloud.

"One or two absurd little reasons: because I was staying in his house; because you were engaged to him; because, in spite of all temptations, one does one's poor best to remain more or less a gentleman."

"Then why did you go with the policemen?"

"To see what happened. I don't honestly remember making a single comment, much less the least suggestion; if I did it was involuntary, for I went upon the clear understanding with myself that I must say nothing, whatever I might think. I was a mere spectator—immensely interested—fascinated, in fact—but as close as wax, if you'll believe me."

Moya did believe him. She knew the family faults; they were bounded by the family virtues, and double-dealing was not within the pale. And Moya felt interested herself; she wished to hear on what pretext Rigden had been arrested; she had already heard that it was slender.

"Tell me what happened."

Theodore was nothing loth: indeed his day in the bush had been better than Moya's, more exciting and unusual, yet every whit as typical in its way. Spicer had led them straight to the clay-pans where Rigden had struck his alleged trail, and there sure enough they had found it.

"I confess I could see nothing myself when the tracker first got off; but half a glance was enough for him; and on he went like a blood-hound, with his black muzzle close to the ground, the rest of us keeping a bit behind and well on one side. Presently there's a foot-print I can see for myself, then more that I simply couldn't, then another plain one; and this time Billy—they're all called Billy—simply jumped with joy. At least I thought it was with joy, till I saw him pointing from his own marks to the others, and shaking his black head. Both prints were about the same depth.

"'Him stamp,' says Billy. 'What for him stamp?'

"But we pushed on and came to some soft ground where any white fool could have run down the tracks; and presently they brought us to a fence, which we crossed by strapping down the wires and leading our horses over, but not where Rigden had led his. Well, we lost the tracks eventually where Rigden said he'd lost them, at what they're pleased to call a 'tank' in these parts; the black fellow went round and round the waterhole, but devil another footmark could he find. So then we went back on the tracks we had found. And presently there's a big yabber-yabber on the part of William, who waddles about on the sides of his feet to show his bosses what he means, and turns in his toes like a clown.

"Well, I asked the sergeant what it was all about; but he wouldn't tell me. And it was then that this fellow Spicer began to play the fool: he had smelt the rat himself, I suppose. He made a still greater ass of himself at the fence, where the blackfellow messed about a long time over Rigden's marks when we got back there. After that we all came marching home, or rather riding hell-to-leather. And the fun became fast and furious; so to speak, of course; for I needn't tell you it was no fun for me, Moya."

"Quite sure? Well, never mind; go on."

"There was no end of a row. Harkness and Myrmidons entered the barracks, and Spicer ordered them out. They insisted on searching Rigden's room. Spicer swore they shouldn't, and appealed to me. What could I do, a mere visitor? I remonstrated, advised them to wait, and so forth; further resistance would have been arrant folly; yet that madman Spicer was for holding the fort with the station ordnance!"

"Go on," said Moya again: she had opened her lips to say something else, but the obvious soundness of Theodore's position came home to her in time.

"Well, the long and short of it is that the sergeant came to me on the verandah with the very pair of boots with which the tracks had been made; a heel was off one of them; they were too small for Rigden, yet they were found hidden away in his room. The astounding thing is that the blessed blackfellow had spotted that the tracks were not made by the man to whom the boots belonged. He had turned in his toes and walked on the outside of his feet; it wasn't so with the trail they followed up to these pines yesterday; and diamond had cut diamond about as neatly as you could wish to see it done. It was smart of Rigden to run alongside his horse and make it look as though he were riding alongside the trail; but it wouldn't do for the wily savage, and I'm afraid the result will be devilish unpleasant."

There was no fear, however, in the clean-cut and clean-shaven face, nor did Theodore's tone suggest any possible unpleasantness to him or his. Moya could have told him so in a manner worthy of himself, but again she showed some self-restraint, and was content to thank him briefly for putting her in possession of all the facts.

"Ah!" said Theodore, "I only wish I could do that! You talked a little while ago about my suspecting the truth; well, I give you my word that I haven't even yet the ghost of an idea what the real truth can be."

"You mean as to motive?"

"Exactly. Why on earth should he risk his all to save the skin of a runaway convict? What can that convict be to him, Moya? Or is the sole explanation mere misplaced, chuckle-headed chivalry?"

"What should you say?" asked Moya quietly.

"I'll tell you frankly," said Theodore at once; "as things were I should have hesitated, but as things are there's no reason why I shouldn't say what I think. It's evidently some relation; a man only does that sort of thing for his flesh and blood. Now do you happen to remember, when this—I mean to say that—engagement was more or less in the air, that some of us rather wanted to know who his father was? Not that—"

"I know," Moya interrupted; "I'm not likely to forget it. So that's what you think, is it?"

"I do; by Jove I do! Wouldn't you say yourself—"

"No, I wouldn't; and no more need you. What are your ideas, by the way, if this is not the ghost of one? I congratulate you upon it from that point of view, if from no other!"

Theodore stuck a fresh cigarette between his lips, and struck the match with considerable vigour. It is not pleasant to be blown from one's own petard, or even scathed in one's own peculiar tone of offence.

"I simply wanted to spare your feelings, my dear girl," was the rejoinder, the last three words being thrown in for the special irritation of Moya. "Not that I see how it can matter now."

The special irritant ceased to gall.

"Now!" echoed Moya. "What do you mean by now?"

"Why, the whole thing's off, of course."

"What whole thing?"

"Your late engagement."

"Oh, is it! Thanks for the news; it's the first I've heard of it."

"Then it won't be the last. You're not going to marry a convict's son, or a convict either; and this fellow promises to be both."

"I shall marry exactly whom I like," said Moya, trembling.

"Don't flatter yourself! You may say so out of bravado, but you're the last person to make a public spectacle of yourself; especially when—well, you know, to put it brutally, this is pretty well bound to ruin him, whatever else it does or does not. Besides, you don't like him any more; you've stopped even thinking you do. Do you suppose I've got no eyes?"

"Theodore," said Moya in a low voice, "if I were your wife I'd murder you!"

"Oh, no, you wouldn't; and meanwhile don't talk greater rot than you can help, Moya. Believe me it isn't either the time or the place. We must get out of the place, by the way, the first thing to-morrow. I see you're still wearing his ring. The sooner you take that off and give it to me to return to him the better."

"It will come to that," said Moya's heart; "but not through Theodore; no, thank you!"

"It shall never come to it at all!" replied her heart of hearts.

And her lips echoed the "Never!" as she marched to the door. Theodore had his foot against it in time.

"Now listen to me! No, you're not going till you listen to reason and me! You may call me a brute till you're black in the face. I don't mind being one for your own good. This thing's coming to an end; in fact it's come; it ought never to have begun, but I tell you it's over. The family were always agreed about it, and I'm practically the head of the family; at all events I'm acting head up here, and I tell you this thing's over whether you like it or not. But you like it. What's the good of pretending you don't? But whether you do or you don't you shall never marry the fellow! And now you know it you may go if you like. Only do for God's sake be ready in the morning, like the sane person you always used to be."

Moya did not move an inch towards the opened door. Her tears were dry; fires leapt in their stead.

"Is that all?"

"Unless you wish me to say more."

"What a fool you are, Theodore!"

"I'm afraid I distrust expert evidence."

"With all your wits you don't know the first thing about women!"

"You mean that you require driving like Paddy's pig? Oh, no, you don't, Moya; go and sleep upon it."

"Sleep!"

It was one burst of all she felt, but only one.

"I'm afraid you won't," said Theodore, with more humanity. "Still it's better to lose a night thinking things over, calmly and surely, as you're very capable of doing, than to go another day with that ring upon your finger."

Moya stared at him with eyes in which the fires were quenched, but not by tears. She looked dazed.

"Do put your mind to it—your own sane mind!" her brother pleaded, with more of wisdom than he had shown with her yet. "And—I don't want to be hard—I never meant to be hard about this again—but God help you now to the only proper and sensible decision!"

So was he beginning to send his juries about their vital business; and, after all, Moya went to hers with as much docility as the twelve good men and true.

Theodore was right about one thing. She must put her mind to it once and for ever.

CHAPTER XII

AN ESCAPADE

She put her mind to it with characteristic thoroughness and honesty. Let there be no mistake about Moya Bethune. She had faults of temper, and faults of temperament, and as many miscellaneous faults as she was quick to find in others; but this did not retard her from seeing them in herself. She was a little spoilt; it is the almost inevitable defect of the popular qualities. She had a good conceit of herself, and a naughty tongue; she could not have belonged to that branch of the Bethunes and quite escaped either. On the other hand, she was not without their cardinal merits. There was, indeed, a brutal honesty in the breed; in Moya it became a singular sincerity, not always pleasing to her friends, but counterbalanced by the brightness and charm of her personality. She was incapable of deceiving another; infinitely rarer, she was equally incapable of deceiving herself; and could consider most things from more standpoints than are accessible to most women, always provided that she kept that cornerstone of all sane judgment, her temper. She had lost it with Rigden and lost it with Theodore, and was in a pretty bad temper with herself to boot; but that is a minor matter; it does not drive the blood to the brain; it need not obscure every point of view but one. And there were but two worthy of Moya's consideration.

There was her own point of view, and there was Rigden's. Moya took first innings; she was the woman, after all.

She began with the beginning of this visit—this visit that the almanac pretended was but fifty hours old after all these days and nights: Well, to believe it, and go back to the first night: they had been happy enough then, still happier next day, happiest of all in the afternoon. Moya could see the shadows and feel the heat, and hear Rigden wondering whether she would ever care for the place, and her own light-hearted replies; but there she checked herself, and passed over the memorable end of that now memorable conversation, and took the next phase in due order.

Of course she had been angry; anybody of any spirit, similarly placed, would have resented being deserted by the hour together for the first wayfarer. And the lie made it worse; and the refusal to explain matters made the lie incalculably worse. He had put her in an abominable position, professing to love her all the time. How could she believe in such love? Love and trust were inseparable in her mind. Yet he had not trusted her for a moment; even when she stooped to tell a lie herself, to save him, even then he could not take her into his confidence. It was the least he could have done after that; it was the very least that she had earned.

Most of the next day—to-day!—even Moya shirked. Why had it laid such a hold upon her—the bush— the bush life—the whole thing? Was it the mere infection of a real enthusiasm? Or was it but the meretricious glamour of the foregone, and would the fascination have been as great if all had still been well? Moya abandoned these points; they formed a side issue after all. Her mind jumped to the final explanation—still ringing in her ears. It was immeasurably worse than all the rest, in essence, in significance, in result. The result mattered least; there was little weakness in Moya; she would have snapped her fingers at the world for the man she loved. But how could she forgive his first deceit, his want of trust in her to the end? And how could she think for another moment of marrying a man whom she could not possibly forgive?

She did not think of it. She relinquished her own point of view, and tried with all her honesty to put herself in his place instead.

It was not very difficult. The poverty-stricken childhood (so different from her own!) with its terrible secret, its ever-hidden disgrace; small wonder if it had become second nature to him to hide it! Then there was the mother. Moya had always loved him for the tone of his lightest reference to his mother. She thought now of the irreparable loss of that mother's death, and felt how she herself had sworn in her heart to repair it. She thought of their meeting, his sunburnt face, the new atmosphere he brought with him, their immediate engagement: the beginning had come almost as quickly as the end! Then

Moya darkened. She remembered how her people had tried to treat him, and how simply and sturdily he had borne himself among them. Whereas, if he had told them all ... but he might have told her!

Yet she wondered. The father was as good as dead, was literally dead to the world; partly for his sake, perhaps, the secret had been kept so jealously all these years by mother and son. Moya still thought that an exception should have been made in her case. But, on mature reflection, she was no longer absolutely and finally convinced of this. And the mere shadow of a doubt upon the point was her first comfort in all these hours.

Such was the inner aspect; the outward and visible was grave enough. It was one thing to be true to a prisoner and a prisoner's son, but another thing to remain engaged to him. Moya was no hand at secrets. And now she hated them. So her mind was made up on one point. If she forgave him, then no power should make her give him up, and she would wear his ring before all her world, though it were the ring of a prisoner in Pentridge Stockade. But she knew what that would mean, and a brief spell of too vivid foresight, which followed, cannot be said to have improved Rigden's chances of forgiveness.

There was one thing, however, which Moya had unaccountably forgotten. This was the sudden inspiration which had come to her an hour ago, among the station pines. She was reminded of it and of other things by the arrival of Mrs. Duncan with a tray; she had even forgotten that her last meal had been made in the middle of the afternoon, at the rabbiter's camp. Mrs. Duncan had discovered this by questioning young Ives, and the tea and eggs were the result of a consultation with Mr. Bethune.

"And after that," smiled Moya, "you will leave me for the night, won't you? I feel as if I should never want to get up again!"

"I'm sure you do, my dear," the good woman cried.

"I shall lock my door," said Moya. "Don't let anybody come to me in the morning; beg my brother not to come."

"Indeed I'll see he doesn't."

And Mrs. Duncan departed as one who had been told little but who guessed much, with a shake of her head, and a nod to follow in case there was nothing to shake it over; for she was entirely baffled.

Moya locked the door on her.

"To think I should have forgotten! My one hope—my one!"

And she ate every morsel on the tray; then undressed and went properly to bed, for the sake of the rest. But to sleep she was afraid, lest she might sleep too long. And between midnight and dawn, she was not only up once more, but abroad by herself in the darkest hour.

Her door she left locked behind her; the key she pushed underneath; and she stepped across the verandah with her riding habit gathered up in one hand, and both shoes clutched in the other.

"It is dreadful! I am as bad as he is. But I can't help it. There's nobody else to do it for me—unless I tell them first. And at least I can keep his secret!"

The various buildings lay vague and opaque in the darkness: not a spark of light in any one of them. And the moon had set; the stars alone lit Moya to the horse-yard.

Luckily she was not unused to horses. She not only had her own hack at home, but made a pet of it and kept her eye upon the groom. A single match, blown out in an instant, showed Moya the saddle and bridle which she had already used, with a water-bag hanging hard by, in the hut adjoining the yard. The bag she filled from the tank outside. The rest was an even simpler matter; a rocking-horse could not have stood quieter than the bony beast which Ives had left behind with the night-horse.

It proved a strong and stolid mount, with a hard, unyielding, but methodical canter, and only one bad habit: it shaved trees and gateposts a little too closely for a rider unaccustomed to the bush. Moya was near disaster at the start; thereafter she allowed for the blemish, and crossed Butcher-boy without mishap.

It was now the darkest quarter of the darkest hour; and Moya was quite thankful that she had no longer a track to follow or to lose. For in Big Bushy she turned sharply to the left, as in the morning with young Ives, and once more followed the fence; but this time she hugged it, and was not happy unless she could switch the wires to make certain they were there.

It was lighter when she reached the first corner: absolute blackness had turned to a dark yet transparent grey; it was as though the ink had been watered; but in a little it was ink no more. Moya turned in her saddle, and a broadening flail of bloodshot blue was sweeping the stars one by one out of the eastern sky.

Also Moya felt the wind of her own travelling bite shrewdly through her summer blouse; and she put a stop to the blundering, plodding canter about half-way down the east-and-west fence whose eastern angle contained the disused whim and hut.

It was no longer necessary to switch the wires; even the line of trees in Blind Man's Block had taken shape behind them; and that sinister streak soon stood for the last black finger-mark of the night.

Further down the fence a covey of crows got up suddenly with foul outry; and Moya, remembering the merino which had fallen by the way, steeled her body once more to the bony one's uneasy canter.

The beast now revealed itself a dapple-grey; and at last between its unkempt ears, and against the slaty sky to westward, Moya described the timbers of the whim.

She reined in again, her bent head puzzling over what she should say.

And again she cantered, the settled words upon her lips; but there they were destined to remain until forgotten; for it was at this point that Moya's adventure diverged alike from her purpose and her preconception.

In the first place the hut was empty. It took Moya some minutes to convince herself of the fact. Again and again she called upon the supposed occupant to come out declaring herself a friend come to warn him, as indeed she had. At last she dismounted and entered, her whip clutched firmly, her heart in her mouth. The hut was without partition or inner chamber. A glance proved it as empty as it had seemed.

Moya was nonplussed: all her plans had been built upon the supposition that she should find the runaway still skulking in the hut where she had seen him the previous forenoon. She now perceived how groundless her supposition had been; it seemed insane when she remembered that the runaway had as certainly seen her—and her sudden flight at sight of him. Unquestionably she had made a false start. Yet she did not see what else she could have done.

She led her horse to the whim itself. Twin shafts ran deep into the earth, side by side like the barrels of a gun. But this whim was finally forsaken; the long rope and the elaborate buckets had been removed and stored; and the slabbed shafts ended in tiny glimmering squares without break or foot-hole from brink to base.

Moya stood still to think; and very soon the thought of the black tracker put all others out of court. It came with a sigh: if only she had him there! He would think nothing of tracking the fugitive from the hut whithersoever his feet had carried him; was it only the blacks who could do such things?

How would he begin? Moya recalled her brother's description, and thought she knew. He would begin by riding down the fence, and seeing if anybody had crossed it.

She was doing this herself next minute. And the thought that had come with a sigh had already made her heart beat madly, and the breath come quicker and quicker through her parted lips; but not with fear; she was much too excited to feel a conscious qualm. Besides, she had somehow no fear of the unhappy man, his father.

Excitement flew to frenzy when she actually found the place. She knew it on the instant, and was never in doubt. There were several footmarks on either side of the fence; on the far side a vertebrate line of them, pointing plainly to the scrub; even her unskilled eye could follow it half the way.

The next thing was to strap down the wires, but Moya could not wait for that. She galloped to a gate that she had seen in the corner near the whim, and came up the other side of the fence also at a gallop.

The trail was easily followed to the scrub: among the trees the ground was harder and footprints proportionately faint. By dismounting, however, and dropping her handkerchief at each apparent break of the chain, Moya always succeeded in picking up the links eventually. Now they gave her no trouble for half-an-hour; now a check would last as long again; but each half-hour seemed like five minutes in her excitement. The trees grew thicker and thicker, but never any higher. Their branches swept the ground and interlaced; and many were the windings of the faint footmarks tenaciously followed by Moya and the dapple-grey. They were as divers wandering on the bed of a shallow sea; for all its shallowness, the patches of sunlight were fewer and fewer, and farther between; if they were also hotter, Moya did not notice the difference. She did not realize into what a labyrinth she was penetrating. Her entire attention was divided between the last footprint and the next; she had none over for any other consideration whatsoever. It was an extreme instance of the forcing of one faculty at the expense of all the rest. Moya thought no more even of what she should say when she ran her man to earth. She had decided all that before she reached the hut. No pang of hunger or of thirst assailed her; excitement and concentration were her meat and drink.

Yet when the end came her very first feeling was that of physical faintness and exhaustion. But then it was an exceedingly sudden and really terrifying end. Moya was dodging boles and ducking under branches, the dapple-grey behind her, her arm through the reins, when all at once these tightened. Moya turned quickly, thinking the horse was unable to follow.

It was.

A gnarled hand, all hair and sinew, held it by the bridle.

CHAPTER XIII

BLIND MAN'S BLOCK

It was some moments before Moya looked higher than that hand, and it prepared her for a worse face than she found waiting for her own. The face was fierce enough, and it poured a steady fire upon the girl from black eyes blazing in the double shade of a felt wideawake and the overhanging mallee. But it was also old, and lined, and hunted; the man had grown grey in prison; whatever his offences, there was rare spirit in a last dash for freedom at his age. Moya had not thought so before. She was surprised that she should think it now. The last thing that she had expected to feel was an atom of real sympathy with the destroyer of her happiness. And yet it was the first thing she felt.

"Please don't look at me like that," she begged. "I wish you no harm, believe me!"

There was a pause, and then a first stern question.

"Who sent you here?"

"Nobody."

"Rot!"

"It's the truth."

"How else did you find me?"

"I saw you yesterday in the hut; you know that; you saw me."

"This is not the hut."

"No, but as you weren't there I looked for your tracks. And I found them. And here I am."

Shaggy brows rose above the piercing eyes.

"I thought you didn't come from the bush?"

"Nor do I; but I have heard a good deal about tracking, this last day or two; and I had luck."

"You've come all this way alone?"

"Absolutely."

"Then nobody else knows anything about it. That's certain. But they will know! You'll be followed, and I shall be found!"

"I don't think so; they'll think I've gone somewhere else."

The convict gave her a long look, and his hawk's eye gleamed; then he turned his attention to the dapple-grey. It was over a minute before he spoke again.

"Do you know who I am?" he then asked.

"Captain Bovill."

He smiled wickedly.

"And nothing else?"

"Oh, yes," said Moya, sadly; "I know what else you are, of course. His father!"

"So he's had the pluck to tell you, after all?"

"He should have told me at once."

"And lost you?"

"He hasn't lost me yet!" cried Moya impulsively, but from her loyal heart none the less.

"Then why break away from him like this? Wasn't his word good enough?"

"I haven't broken away," said Moya, "from him. I couldn't. I've come to tell you why. They've taken him to prison!"

"Taken him!"

"On your account. They know he helped you. That's all they do know."

The convict stared; but, in the perpetual twilight of the mallee that was the only fact to which Moya could have sworn. She could make nothing of the old man's expression. When he spoke, however, there was no mistaking his tone. It was hard and grim as a prison bell.

"In his turn!" said he. "Well, it'll teach him what it's like."

"But it isn't his turn," cried Moya, in a fury; "what has he done to deserve such degradation, except a good deal more than his duty by you? And this is all the thanks he gets! As though he had taken after you! How can you speak like that of him? How dare you—to me?"

So Moya could turn upon the whilom terror of a colony, a desperado all his days, yet surely never more desperate than now; and her rings flashed, and her eyes flashed, and there was no one there to see! No soul within many miles but the great criminal before her, whose turn it was to astonish Moya. He uncovered; he jerked a bow that was half a shrug, but the more convincing for the blemish; and thereafter hung his cropped head in strange humility.

"You're right!" said he. "I deserve all you've said, and more. He has treated me ten thousand times better than I deserve, and that's my gratitude! Yet if you had been half a lifetime in the hulks—in irons—chained down like a wild beast—why, you'd be one, even you!"

"I know," said Moya in a low voice. "It is terrible to think of!"

"And God bless you for admitting that much," the old man whined, "for it's few that will. Break the law, and the law breaks you—on a wheel! Talk about the wrongs of prisoners; they have neither wrongs nor rights in the eyes of the law; it's their own fault for being prisoners, and that's the last word."

"It is very terrible," said Moya again.

"Ah, but you little know how bad it is; and I'm not going to tell you. It's worse than your worst dreams, and that must do for you. The floggings, the irons, the solitary confinement in your irons with the blood running down your back! No, I said I wouldn't, and I won't. But it's hard to hold your tongue when you're talking to a lady for the first time in thirty years. And to think of a young lady like you coming all this way, alone too, to say a kind word to a double-dyed old rogue like me! It's the most wonderful thing I ever heard of in all my days. I can't think why you did it, for the life of me I can't!"

"It was to tell you about your son," Moya reminded him.

"Ah, poor fellow! God help him, for I can't."

"Are you quite sure?" said Moya gently, and for once rather nervously as well.

"Sure? Of course I'm sure! Why, what can I do?" cried the other, with sudden irritation as suddenly suppressed. "Hiding—hunted—with every hand against me but yours—I'd help him if I could, but I can't."

"So he's to go to prison instead of you?"

Moya spoke quietly, but with the more effect; indeed, she was herself beginning to feel surprised at her success with a desperate man in vital straits. He was more amenable than she had imagined possible. That he should parley with her at all was infinite encouragement. But now there came a pause.

"I see what you're driving at," he cried savagely at last. "You want me to give myself up! I'll see you—further."

The oath was dropped at the last moment—another strange sign—but the tone could not have been stronger. Yet the mere fact that he had seen her point, and made it for her, filled Moya with increasing confidence.

"I don't wonder," she had the tact to say. "How could you be expected to go back—to that—of your own free will? And yet what can be worse than waiting—waiting till—"

"I'm taken, eh? Is that what you want to say? They shall never take me alive, curse them; don't you trouble about that!"

The tone was stubborn, ferocious, blood-curdling, but at least it was in keeping with the blazing eyes and the great jowl beneath. Moya looked steadily at the bushranger, the mutineer, the indomitable criminal of other days; more remained of him than she had fancied. And to think that he had soft answers for her!

She made haste to earn another.

"Please—please—don't speak like that! It is dreadful. And I feel sure there is some middle course."

"I'm no believer in middle courses!"

"That I know. Yet—you have suffered so—I feel sure something could be done! I—that is my people—have influence—money—"

"They can keep their money."

Moya begged his pardon. It was not an act in which she excelled. Yet nothing could have been sweeter than her confusion, nothing finer than her frank humility.

"I was only wondering if there was anything—anything—we could any of us do! It would be understood so well. His father! Surely that would be enough! I know the Governor. I would think nothing of going to him. I honestly believe that he would pardon you both!"

Moya felt the black eyes burning, and for once her own eyes fell; indeed she was a wondrous picture of beauty and youth and enthusiasm, there in that place, in her dainty blouse and habit, with the dull green mallee above and all around her. But they were a yet more extraordinary pair, the old bushranger of a bygone day, and the Melbourne beauty of the present.

"So you believe that, do you?" said the former sardonically.

"From the bottom of my heart."

"Suppose you were wrong?"

"I would move heaven and earth."

"Then jump on your horse!"

"Why?"

"I'm coming with you—to the police-barracks!"

It was like a dream. Moya could have rubbed her eyes, and soon had to do so, for they were full of tears. She sobbed her thanks; she flung out both hands to press them home. The convict waited grimly at her horse's head.

"Better wait and see what comes of it," said he. "And think yourself lucky worse hasn't come of it yet! I'm not thinking of myself; do you know where you are? Do you know that this is Blind Man's Block? Haven't you heard about it? Then you should thank your stars you've a good old bushman to lead you out; for it's like getting out of a maze, I can tell you; and if you'd been warned, as I was, I don't think you'd have ventured in."

Moya had never realised that it was into Blind Man's Block she had plunged so rashly. Nor did the discovery disturb her now. She was too full of her supreme triumph to dwell for many moments upon any one of the risks that she had run for its accomplishment. Neither did she look too far ahead. She would keep faith with this poor creature; no need to count the cost just yet. Moya set her mind's eye upon the reunion at the police-barracks: her advent as the heroine of a bloodless victory, her intercession for the father, her meeting with the son.

The prospect dazzled her. It had its gravely precarious aspect. But one thing at a time. She had done her best; no ultimate ill could come of it; of that she felt as certain as of the fact that she was sitting in her saddle and blindly following an escaped criminal through untrodden wilds.

Suddenly she discovered that she was not doing this exactly. She had not consciously diverged, and yet her leader was bearing down upon her with a scowl.

"Why don't you follow me?" he cried. "Do you want to get bushed in Blind Man's Block?"

"I wasn't thinking," replied Moya. "It must have been the horse."

Bovill seized the bridle.

"It's a fool of a horse!" said he. "Why, we're quite close to the fence, and it wants to head back into the middle of the block!"

Moya remarked that she did not recognise the country.

"Of course you don't," was the reply. "You came the devil of a round, but I'm taking you straight back to the fence. Trust an old hand like me; I can smell a fence as a sheep smells water. You trust yourself to me!"

Moya had already done so. It was too late to reconsider that. Yet she did begin to wonder somewhat at herself. That hairy hand upon the bridle, it lay also rather heavily on her nerves. And the mallee shrub showed no signs of thinning; the open spaces were as few as ever, and as short; on every hand the leaves seemed whispering for miles and miles.

"We're a long time getting to that fence," said Moya at length.

The convict stopped, looked about him in all directions, and finally turned round. In doing so his right hand left the bridle, but in an instant the other was in its place. Moya, however, was too intent upon his face to notice this.

"I'm afraid I've missed it," said he calmly.

"Missed the fence?"

"It looks like it."

"After what you said just now? Oh, what a fool I was to trust you!"

Their eyes were joined for the next few seconds; then the man's face relaxed in a brutal grin. And Moya began to see the measure of her folly.

"Hypocrite!" she gasped.

"Don't call names, my dear. It's not kind, especially to your father-in-law that is to be!"

Moya shuddered in every member except the hand that gripped her whalebone switch. The gold-mounted handle was deep in her flesh.

"Leave go of my bridle," she said quietly.

"Not just yet, my dear."

The whalebone whistled through the air, and came slashing down upon the dapple-grey's neck, within an inch of the hairy fingers, which were nevertheless snatched away. Moya had counted on this and its result. The animal was off at its best pace; but the desperate hands grabbed Moya's habit as it passed, and in another instant she was on the ground. In yet another she had picked herself up, but she never even looked for the horse; she fixed her eye upon her loathly adversary as on a wild beast; and now he looked nothing else, with canine jaw and one vile lip protruding, and hell's own fire in his wicked eyes.

Luckily her grip of the riding-whip had tightened, not relaxed; but now she held it as a sword; and it helped her to cow a brute who had the real brute's dread of the lash. But also she was young and supple, and the man was old. The contrast had never been so sharp; for now they were both in their true colours; and every vileness of the one was met by its own antithesis in the other. It was will against will, personality against personality, in an open space among the mallee and the full glare of a climbing sun, mile upon mile from human help or habitation. And the battle was fought to a finish without a word.

Moya only heard a muttering as the wretch swung round upon his heel, and walked after the dapple-grey, which had come to a standstill within sight. But she was not done with the blackguard yet. She watched him remove the lady's saddle, then carefully detach the water-bag, and sling it about himself by means of the stirrup-leather. Then he mounted, bare-back; but Moya knew that he would not abandon her without his say; and she was waiting for him with the self-same eye that had beaten him off.

He reined up and cursed her long and filthily. Her ear was deaf to that; but little of it conveyed the slightest meaning; her unchanged face declared as much. So then he trimmed his tongue accordingly.

"Sorry to take the water-bag; but through you I've forgot mine and my swag too. Better try and find 'em; they're away back where I camped last night; you're welcome to the drop that's left, if there is one. You look a bit black about the gills as it is. Have a drop to show there's no ill-feeling before I go."

And he dangled the bag before her, meaning to whisk it back again. But Moya disappointed him. She was parched with thirst, though she only realised it now. She neither spoke nor moved a muscle.

"Then die of thirst, and be damned to you! Do you know where you are? Blind Man's Block—Blind Man's Block! Don't you forget it again, because I shan't be here to remind you; a horse was what I wanted, and was promised, so you're only keeping that poor devil's word for him. Give him my blessing if you ever see him again; but you never will. They say it's an easy place to die in, this here Blind Man's Block, but you'll see for yourself. A nice little corpse we'll make, won't we? But we'll die and rot the same, and the crows'll have our eyes for breakfast and our innards for dinner! And do you good, you little white devil, you!"

Moya remained standing in the same attitude, with the same steady eye and the same marble pallor, long after the monster disappeared, and the last beat of the dapple-grey's hoofs was lost among the normal wilds of the bush. Then all at once a great light leapt to her face. But it was not at anything that she had heard or seen; it was at something which had come to her very suddenly in the end. And for a long time after that, though lost and alone in Blind Man's Block, and only too likely to die the cruel death designed for her, Moya Bethune was a happier woman than she had been for many an hour.

CHAPTER XIV

HIS OWN COIN

"Cooo-eee!"

It was a far cry and faint, so faint that Moya was slow to believe her ears. She had not stirred from the scene of her late encounter, but this inactivity was not without design. Moya was tired out already; she had too much sense to waste her remaining strength upon the heat of the day. She found the chewing of leaves avert the worst pangs of thirst, so long as she remained in the shade, and there she determined to rest for the present. Sooner or later she would be followed and found, and the fewer her wanderings, the quicker and easier that blessed consummation. Her plight was still perilous enough, and Moya did not blink this fact any more than others. Yet another fact there was, of which she was finally convinced, though she had yet to prove it; meanwhile the mere conviction was her stay and comfort. She was gloating over it, a leaf between her dry lips, and her aching body stretched within reach of more leaves, when she thought she heard the coo-ee.

She sat up and listened. It came again. And this time Moya was sure.

She sprang to her feet, and, deliverance within hail, realised her danger for the first time fully. Sunburnt hands put a trembling trumpet to her lips, and out came a clearer call than had come to Moya.

The answer sounded hoarse, and was as far away as ever; but prompt enough; and now Moya was as sure of the direction as of the sound itself. Nor had she occasion to coo-ee any more. For the first thing she saw, perhaps a furlong through the scrub, was a riderless horse, bridled but unsaddled, with a forefoot through the reins.

True to its unpleasant habit, the dapple-grey had done noble service to the human race, by swerving under a branch at full gallop, and scraping its rider into space.

The wretch lay helpless in the sun, with a bloody forehead and an injured spine. Moya's water-bag had fallen clear, and lay out of his reach by a few inches which were yet too many for him to move. He demanded it as soon as she came up, but with an oath, and Moya helped herself first, drinking till her hands came close together upon the wet canvas.

"Now you can finish it," she said, "if you're such a fool. I've left you more than you deserve."

He cursed her hideously, and a touch of unmerited compassion came upon her as she discovered how really helpless he was. So she held his head while he drained the last drop, and as it fell back he cursed her again, but began whining when she made off without a word.

"My back must be broken—I've no feeling in my legs. And you'd let me die alone!"

"Your own coin," said Moya, turning at her distance.

"It wasn't. I swear it wasn't. I swear to God I was only doing it to frighten you! I was going for help."

"How can you tell such lies?" asked Moya sternly.

"They're not, they're the solemn truth, so help me God!"

"You're only making them worse; own they are lies, or I'm off this minute."

"Oh, they are then, damn you!"

Only the oath was both longer and stronger.

"Swear again, and it won't be this minute, it'll be this very second!" cried Moya decisively. "So own, without swearing, that you did mean me to die of thirst, so far as you were concerned."

"You never would have done it, though; they'll be on your track by this time."

"That may be. It doesn't alter what you did."

"I offered you a drink, didn't I? It was my only chance to take the horse and the water-bag. I meant to frighten you, but that's all. And now I'm half mad with pain and heat; you'd swear yourself if you were in my shoes; and I can't even feel I've got any on!"

Moya drew a little nearer.

"Nearer, miss—nearer still! Come and stand between me and the sun. Just for a minute! It's burning me to hell!"

Moya took no notice of the word, nor yet of the request.

"Before I do any more for you," said she, "you must tell me the truth."

"I have!"

"Oh, no, you haven't: not the particular truth I want to know. I know it already. Still I mean to hear it from you. It's the truth on quite a different matter; that's what I want," said Moya, and stood over the poor devil as he desired, so that at last the sun was off him, though now he had Moya's eyes instead. "I—I wonder you can't guess—what I've guessed!" she added after a pause.

But she also wondered at something else, for in that pause the blood-stained face had grown ghastlier than before, and Moya could not understand it. The man was so sorely stricken that recapture must now be his liveliest hope: why then should he fear a discovery more or less? And it was quite a little thing that Moya thought she had discovered; a little thing to him, not to her; and she proceeded to treat it as such.

"You know you're not Captain Bovill at all," she told him, in the quiet voice of absolutely satisfied conviction.

"Who told you that?" he roared, half raising himself for the first time, and the fear and fury in his eyes were terrible to see.

"Nobody."

"Ah!"

"But I know it all the same. I've known it this last half-hour. And if I hadn't I should know it now. I see it—where I ought to have seen it from the first—in your face."

"You mean because my son's not the dead spit of his father? But he never was; he took after his mother; he'll tell you that himself."

"It's not what I meant," said Moya, "though it is through the man you call your son that I know he is nothing of the kind. His father may have been a criminal; he was something else first; he would not have left a woman to perish of thirst in the bush, a woman who had done him no harm—who only wished to befriend him—who was going to marry his son!"

There were no oaths to this; but the black eyes gleamed shrewdly in the blood-stained face, and the conical head wagged where it lay.

"You never were in the hulks, you see," said the convict; "else you'd know. No matter what a man goes in, they all come out alike, brute beasts every one. I'm all that, God help me! But I'm the man—I'm the man. Do you think he'd have held out a finger to me if I hadn't been?"

"I've no doubt you convinced him that you were."

"How can one man convince another that he's his father?"

"I don't know. I only know that you have done it."

"Why, he knew me at once!"

"Nonsense! He had never seen you before; he doesn't remember his father."

"Do you suppose he hasn't seen pictures, and heard plenty? No, no; all the rest's a true bill; but Captain Bovill I've lived, and Captain Bovill I'm going to die."

Moya looked at him closely. She could not help shuddering. He saw it, and the fear of death laid hold of him, even as he sweltered in the heat.

"With a lie on your lips?" said Moya, gravely.

"It's the truth!"

"You know it isn't. Own it, for your own sake! Who can tell how long I shall be gone?"

"You shan't go! You shan't go!" he snarled and whined at once. And he clutched vainly at her skirts, the effort leaving him pale as death, and in as dire an agony.

"I must," said Moya. "There's the horse; the saddle's quite near; you shall have all the help that I can bring you, with all the speed that's possible."

She moved away, and the ruthless sun played on every inch of him once more.

"I'm burning—burning!" he yelled. "Have I been in hell upon earth all these years to go to hell itself before I die? Move me, for Christ's sake! Only get me into the shade, and I'll confess—I'll confess!"

Moya tried; but it was terrible; he shrieked with agony, foaming at the mouth, and beating her off with feeble fists. So then she flung herself bodily on an infant hop-bush, and actually uprooted it. And with this and some mallee-branches she made a gunyah over him, though he said it stifled him, and complained bitterly to the end. At the end of all Moya knelt at his feet.

"Now keep your promise."

"What promise?" he asked with an oath, for Moya had been milder than her word.

"You said you would confess."

"Confess what?" he cried, a new terror in his eyes. "I'm not going to die! I don't feel like dying! I've no more to confess!"

"Oh, yes, you have—that you're not his father—nor yet Captain Bovill."

"But I tell you I am. Why—" and the pallid face lit up suddenly—"even the police know that, and you know that they know it!"

It was a random shot, but it made a visible mark, for in her instinctive certainty of the main fact Moya was only now reminded that Rigden himself had told her the same thing. Her discomfiture, however, was but momentary; she held obstinately to her intuition. The police might know it. She knew better than the police; and looking upon their quarry, and going over everything as she looked, came in a flash upon a fresh theory and a small fact in its support.

"Then they don't know who it is they're after!" cried Moya. "You're not even their man; his eyes were brown; it was in the description; but yours are the blackest I ever saw."

It was not a good point. He might well make light of it. But it was enough for Moya and her woman's instinct; or so she said, and honestly thought for the moment. She was less satisfied when she had caught the horse and still must hear the mangled man; for he railed at her, from the gunyah she had built him, to the very end. And to Moya it seemed that there was more of triumph than of terror in his tone.

CHAPTER XV

THE FACT OF THE MATTER

Sergeant Harkness had his barracks to himself. To be sure, the cell was occupied; but, contrary to the usual amenities of the wilderness, such as euchre and Christian names between the sergeant and the ordinary run of prisoners, with this one Harkness would have nothing to do. It was a personal matter between them: the capital charge had divided them less. Constable and tracker had meanwhile been called out on fresh business. That was in the middle of the day. Since then the coach had passed with the mail; and Harkness had been pacing his verandah throughout the sleepiest hour of the afternoon, only pausing to read and re-read one official communication, when Moya's habit fluttered into view towards four o'clock.

"Well, I'm dished!" exclaimed the sergeant. "And alone, too, after all!"

He hastened to meet her.

"Where on earth have you been, Miss Bethune? Do you know there's another search-party out, looking for you this time? My sub and the tracker were fetched this morning. I'd have gone myself only—" and he jerked a thumb towards a very small window at one end of the barracks.

"Mr. Rigden?" said Moya, lowering her voice.

"Yes."

"So you've got him still! I'm glad; but I don't want him to know I'm here. Stay—does he think I'm lost?"

"No. I thought it better not to tell him."

"That was both wise and kind of you, Sergeant Harkness! He must know nothing just yet. I want to speak to you first."

And she urged the dapple-grey, now flagging sorely, towards the other end of the building; but no face appeared at the little barred window; for Rigden was sound asleep in his cell.

"We're all right," said Moya, sliding to the ground; "we stopped at a tank and a boundary-rider's hut, but not the Eureka boundary. I didn't get out the same way I got in, you see—I mean out of the Blind Man's Block."

"Blind Man's Block! Good God! have you been there? You're lucky to have got out at all!"

"It wasn't easy. I thought we should never strike a fence, and when we did I had to follow it for miles before there was a gate or a road. But the boundary-rider was very kind; he not only gave me the best meal I ever had in my life; he set me on the road to you."

Indeed the girl was glowing, though dusty and dishevelled from head to foot. Her splendid colouring had never been more radiant, nor had the bewildered sergeant ever looked upon such brilliant eyes. But it was a feverish brilliance, and a glance would have apprised the skilled observer of a brain in the balance between endurance and suspense.

"What on earth were you doing in Blind Man's Block?" asked Harkness, suspiciously.

"I'll tell you. I'll tell you something else as well! But first you must tell me something, Sergeant Harkness."

"I believe you know where he is," quoth the sergeant, softly.

"Do you know who he is?" cried Moya, coming finely to her point.

Harkness stared harder than ever.

"Well, I thought I did—until this afternoon."

"Who did you think it was?"

"Well, there's no harm in saying now. Rightly or wrongly, I only told Mr. Rigden at the time. But I always thought it was Captain Bovill, the old bushranger who escaped from Pentridge two or three weeks ago."

"Then you thought wrong," said Moya, boldly.

Nevertheless she held her breath.

"So it seems," growled the sergeant.

"Why does it seem so?"

It was a new voice crying, and one so tremulous that Harkness could scarcely recognise it as Miss Bethune's.

"I've heard officially—"

"What have you heard?"

"You see we were all informed of Bovill's escape."

"Go on! Go on!"

"So in the same way we've been advised of his death."

"His—death!"

"Steady, Miss Bethune! There—allow me. We'll get in out of the sun; he won't hear us at this end of the verandah. Here's a chair. That's the ticket! Now, just one moment."

He returned with something in a glass which Moya thought sickening. But it did her good. She ceased giggling and weeping by turns and both at once.

"So he's dead—he's dead! Have you told Mr. Rigden that?"

"No; I'm not seeing much of Mr. Rigden."

"I am glad. I will tell him myself, presently. You will let me, I suppose?"

"Surely, Miss Bethune. There's no earthly reason why he should be here, except his own obstinacy, if you'll excuse my saying so. He was remanded this morning; but Mr. Cross of Strathavon, who signed the warrant yesterday, and came over for the examination this forenoon, not only wanted to take bail, but offered to find it himself. Wanted to carry him off in his own buggy, he did! But Mr. Rigden said here he was, and here he'd stick until his fate was settled. Would you like to see him now?"

"Presently," repeated Moya. "I want to hear more; then I may have something to tell you. When and where did this death occur, and what made you so sure that it was the dead man who came to Eureka? You will understand my questions in a minute."

"Only I must answer them first," said the sergeant, smiling. "I am to give myself clean away, am I?"

"We must all do that sometimes, Sergeant Harkness. It will be my turn directly. Let us trust each other."

Harkness looked into her candid eyes, calmer and more steadfast for their recent tears, and his mind was made up.

"I'll trust you," he said; "you may do as you like about me. Perhaps you yourself have had the wish that's father to the thought, or rather the thought that comes of the wish and nothing else? Well, then, that's what's been the matter with me. The moment I heard of that old rascal's escape, like every other fellow in the force, I yearned to have the taking of him. Of course it wasn't on the cards, hundreds of miles up-country as we are here, besides being across the border; yet when they got clear away, and headed for the Murray, there was no saying where they might or might not cast up. Well, it seems they never reached the Murray at all; but last week down in Balranald I heard a rum yarn about a stowaway aboard one of the Echuca river-steamers; they never knew he was aboard until they heard him go overboard just the other side of Balranald. Then they thought it was one of themselves, until they mustered and found none missing; and then they all swore it was a log, except the man at the wheel who'd seen it; so I pretended to think with the rest—but you bet I didn't! I went down the river on the off-chance, but I never let on who I hoped it might be. And what with a swaggy whose swag had been stolen, and his description of the man who he swore had stolen it, I at last got on the tracks of the man I've lost. He was said to be an oldish man; that seemed good enough; they were both of them oldish men, the two that had escaped."

"The two!" cried Moya in high excitement. "The two! I keep forgetting there were two of them; you see you never said so when you came to the station."

"I wanted to keep it all to myself," confessed the crest-fallen sergeant. "I only told two living men who I thought it was that I was after. One was my sub—who guessed—and the other was Mr. Rigden."

"Were the two men who escaped anything like each other?"

"Well, they were both old lags from the Success, and both superior men at one time; old particulars who'd been chained together, as you might say, for years; and I suppose that sort of thing does beat a man down into a type. However, their friendship didn't go for much when they got outside; for Gipsy Marks murdered Captain Bovill as sure as emu's eggs are emu's eggs!"

"Murdered him!" gasped Moya; and her brain reeled to think of the hours she had spent with the murderer. But all was clear to her now, from the way in which Rigden had been imposed upon in the beginning, to the impostor's obstinate and terrified refusal to own himself as such to the very end.

"Yes, murdered him on the other side of the Murray; the body's only just been found; and meanwhile the murderer's slipped through my fingers," said the sergeant, sourly; "for if it wasn't poor old Bovill I was after, at all events it was Gipsy Marks."

Moya sprang to her feet.

"It was," she cried; "but he hasn't slipped through your fingers at all, unless he's dead. He wasn't when I left him two or three hours ago."

"When you left him?"

"Yes, I found him, and was with him all the morning."

"In Blind Man's Block—with that ruffian?"

"He took my horse and my water-bag, and left me there to die of thirst; but the dear horse turned the tables on him—poor wretch!"

"And you never told me!"

"I am trying to tell you now."

And he let her finish.

But she would not let him go.

"Dear Sergeant Harkness, I can't pretend to have an ounce of pity left for that dreadful being in Blind Man's Block. A murderer, too! At least I have more pity for some one else, and you must let me take him away before you go."

"Impossible, my dear young lady—that is, before communicating with Mr. Cross."

"About bail?"

"Yes."

"What was the amount named this morning?"

"Fifty pounds."

"Give me a sheet of paper and a stamp, and I'll write a cheque myself."

Harkness considered.

"Certainly that could be done," he said at length.

"Then quickly—quickly!"

Yet even when it was done she detained him; even when he put a big key into her hand.

"Must this go further—before the magistrates—after you have found him?"

Harkness hardened.

"The offence is the same. I'm afraid it must."

"It will make it very unpleasant for me," sighed Moya, "when I come up here. And when I've found him for you—and undone anything that was done—though I don't admit that anything was—I—well, I really think you might!"

"Might what?"

"Withdraw the charge!"

"But those tracks weren't his. Mr. Rigden made them. He shouldn't have done that."

"Of course he shouldn't—if he did."

"But of course he did, Miss Bethune. I've known Mr. Rigden for years; we used to be very good friends. I shouldn't speak as I do unless I spoke by the book. But—why on earth did he go and do a thing like that?"

Moya paused.

"If I tell you will you never tell a soul?"

"Never," said the rash sergeant.

"Then he was imposed upon. The wretch pretended he—had some claim—I cannot tell you what. I can tell you no more."

It was provokingly little to have to keep secret for lifetime; yet Harkness was glad to hear even this.

"It was the only possible sort of explanation," said he.

"But it won't explain enough for the world," sighed Moya, so meaningly that the sergeant asked her what she did mean.

"I must really get off," he added.

"Then I'll be plain with you," cried the girl. "Either you must withdraw this charge, and pretend that those tracks were genuine, or I can never come up here to live!"

And she looked her loveliest to emphasise the threat.

"I must see Mr. Rigden about that," was, however, all that Harkness would vouchsafe.

"Very well! That's only fair. Meanwhile—I—trust you, Sergeant Harkness. And I never yet trusted the wrong man!"

That was Moya's last word.

It is therefore a pity that it was not strictly true.

It was a wonderful ride they had together, that ride between the police-barracks and the station, and from drowsy afternoon into cool sweet night. The crickets chirped their welcome on the very boundary, and the same stars came out that Moya had seen swept away in the morning, one by one again. Then the moon came up with a bound, but hung a little as though caught in some pine-trees on the horizon, that seemed scratched upon its disc. And Moya remarked that they were very near home, with such a wealth of tenderness in the supreme word that a mist came over Rigden's eyes.

"Thank God," said he, "that I have lived to hear you call it so, even if it never is to be."

"But it is—it is. Our own dear home!"

"We shall see."

"What do you mean, darling?"

"I am going to tell Theodore the whole thing."

"After I've taken such pains to make it certain that none of them need ever know a word?"

"Yes; he shall know; he can do what he thinks fit about letting it go any further."

Moya was silent for a little.

"You're right," she said at last. "I know Theodore. He'll never breathe it; but he'll think all the more of you, dearest."

"I owe it to him. I owe it to you all, and to myself. I am not naturally a fraud, Moya."

"On the other hand, it was very natural not to speak of such a thing."

"But it was wrong. I knew it at the time. Only I could not risk—"

Moya touched his lips with her switch.

"Hush, sir! That's the one part I shall never—quite—forgive."

"But you have taught me a lesson. I shall never keep another thing back from you in all my life!"

"And I will never be horrid to you again, darling! But of course there will be exceptions to both rules; to yours because there are some things which wouldn't be my business (but this wasn't one of them); to mine, because—well—we none of us have the tempers of angels."

"But you have been my good angel already—and more—so much more!"

They came to the home-paddock gate. The moon was high above the pines. Underneath there were the lesser lights, the earthly lights, but all else was celestial peace.

"I hope they're not looking for me still," said Moya.

"If they are I must go and look for them."

"I won't let you. It's too sweet—the pines—the moonlight—everything."

They rode up to the homestead, with each roof beaming to the moon.

"Not much of a place for the belle of Toorak," sighed Rigden.

"Perhaps not. But, of all places, the place for me!"

"You're as keen as Ives," laughed Rigden as he helped her to dismount. "And I was so afraid the place would choke you off!"

E. W. Hornung – A Short Biography

Ernest William Hornung was born on 7th June 1866 at Cleveland Villas, Marton, Middlesbrough. He was the third son, and youngest of eight children, to John Peter Hornung and his wife Harriet née Armstrong.

By the age of 13 Hornung had joined St Ninian's Preparatory School in Moffat, Dumfriesshire before enrolling at the exclusive Uppingham School, in Rutland, in 1880.

Hornung suffered from a general state of bad health, including asthma and poor eyesight but managed to be well-liked at school and to develop a life-long passion of cricket. He loved to play despite the obvious fact that his talents were rather limited.

At 17 his health worsened, and he left Uppingham to travel to Australia, where a sunnier climate was deemed to be better for his various ailments.

Upon arriving he worked as a tutor to the Parsons family in Mossgiel, in New South Wales. As well as teaching he spent time working in remote sheep stations in the outback and began to contribute materials to the weekly magazine; The Bulletin. It was also at this time that he began work on his first novel.

After two years of very valuable life experiences Hornung returned to England in February 1886, a few months before the death of his father, in November, whose deteriorating business interests had become a constant worry.

Hornung found work in London as a journalist and story writer. In 1887 he published his first story under his own name, 'Stroke of Five', which appeared in Belgravia magazine. His work as a journalist coincided with the reign of terror brought about by Jack the Ripper's grisly murders. From this Hornung developed an interest in criminal behaviour.

He had completed the manuscript of the novel he brought back from Australia and, between July and November 1890, the story, 'A Bride from the Bush', was published in five parts in the respected Cornhill Magazine. It was released later that year in book form. This, his first novel, was well received by critics.

Hoping to further his talents in cricket Hornung, in 1891, became a member of two cricket clubs: the Idlers, whose members included Arthur Conan Doyle and Jerome K. Jerome, and the Strand club.

Hornung knew Doyle's sister, Constance ('Connie') from when he had visited Portugal. Connie was described as attractive, "with pre-Raphaelite looks ... the most sought-after of the Doyle daughters".

They were married on 27th September 1893, although Doyle was not at the wedding and relations between the two writers were occasionally difficult. The Hornung's had their only child, a son, Arthur Oscar (but always called just Oscar), in 1895.

In 1894 Doyle and Hornung began work on a play for Henry Irving, on the subject of boxing; Doyle was, at first, eager to begin and paid Hornung a £50 advance but then withdrew before the first act had been completed: the play was never finished.

Like Hornung's first novel, 'Tiny Luttrell' had Australia as a backdrop and the device of an Australian woman in a culturally alien environment. This theme ran through his next four novels: 'The Boss of Taroomba' (1894), 'The Unbidden Guest' (1894), 'Irralie's Bushranger' (1896), in this Hornung introduced the character of Stingaree, an Oxford-educated, Australian gentleman thief. In 'The Rogue's March' (1896) Hornung began to show a growing fascination with the motivation behind criminal behaviour and was sympathetic to the criminal hero as a victim of events. It was different thinking but caused some consternation for others.

In 1898 Hornung's mother died and he dedicated his next book, a series of short stories; Some Persons Unknown, to her memory.

Later that year Hornung and Connie spent six months in Posillipo, Italy. An account of this trip was published in the May 1899 issue of the Cornhill Magazine.

The fictional character Stingaree was re-written to become his most famous creation; A. J. Raffles; the gentleman thief, first used in six short stories published in 1898 in Cassell's Magazine. Modelled on George Cecil Ives, a Cambridge-educated criminologist and talented cricketer who, like Raffles, lived in the Albany, a gentlemen's only residence in Mayfair. The first tale of the series 'In the Chains of Crime' was published in June that year, titled 'The Ides of March'.

Another account adds to the richness by asserting that Raffles and his sidekick, Bunny Manders, were based not only on Doyle's Holmes and Watson but also on his friends Oscar Wilde and his lover, Lord Alfred Douglas. Whatever the exact amalgam the characters were warmly embraced by the reading public who turned it into both a popular and financial success, although some critics echoed Doyle's own fears of the dubious nature of a criminal being used as a hero.

In early 1899, the Hornung's returned to London, and resided in Pitt Street, West Kensington, for the next six years.

After publishing two novels, 'Dead Men Tell No Tales' (1899) and 'Peccavi' (1900), Hornung published a second collection of Raffles stories, 'The Black Mask', in 1901. The critics again complained about the criminal aspect. The public who bought them had no such qualms.

In 1903 Hornung collaborated with Eugène Presbrey to write a four-act play, 'Raffles, The Amateur Cracksman', which was based on two previously published short stories, 'Gentlemen and Players' and 'The Return Match'. The play was first performed at the Princess Theatre, New York, on 27th October 1903 and ran for 168 performances.

In 1905, after publishing four other books in the interim, Hornung brought back the character Stingaree. Later that year, in response to public demand he published a third collection of Raffles stories in 'A Thief in the Night', in which Manders relates some of the earlier adventures he had had with Raffles.

In 1909 the final Raffles story was published, the full-length novel 'Mr. Justice Raffles'. It was poorly received. The Observer reviewer asking if "Hornung is perhaps a little tired of Raffles".

It seems not. That same year he partnered with Charles Sansom for the play 'A Visit From Raffles', which was performed in November that year at the Brixton Empress Theatre, London.

Hornung turned away from Raffles thereafter, and in February 1911 published 'The Camera Fiend', a thriller whose narrator is an asthmatic cricket enthusiast and his attempts to photograph the soul as it leaves the body. This was followed by 'Fathers of Men' (1912) and 'The Thousandth Woman' (1913) before 'Witching Hill' (1913), a collection of eight short stories in which he introduced the characters Uvo Delavoye and the narrator Gillon. In 1914 his fictional works ceased with 'The Crime Doctor'.

His son, Oscar, left Eton College in 1914, and was due to proceed to King's College, Cambridge later that year. However, the terrors of WWI were about to unleash themselves all over Europe. Oscar volunteered, and was commissioned into the Essex Regiment. He was killed, aged a mere 20, at the Second Battle of Ypres on 6th July 1915.

Although heartbroken Hornung edited and issued privately a collection of Oscar's letters home under the title 'Trusty and Well Beloved', in 1916.

Around this time Hornung himself joined an anti-aircraft unit. He also joined the YMCA and did volunteer work in England for soldiers on leave. In March 1917 he visited France, writing a poem about his experience afterwards—something he had been doing more frequently since Oscar's death—and a collection of his war poetry, 'Ballad of Ensign Joy', was published later that year.

In July 1917 Hornung's poem, 'Wooden Crosses', was published in The Times, and in September, 'Bond and Free' appeared. A few months later he was accepted as a volunteer in a YMCA canteen and library just a few miles behind the Front Line.

Hornung was concerned about support for pacifism among troops and wrote to Connie about it. She spoke to Doyle and, rather than discussing it with Hornung, he informed the military authorities. Hornung was naturally angered by Doyle's action and relations between the two men were further strained as a result. He continued to work at the library until a German offensive overran the British positions and he was forced to retreat, firstly to Amiens and then, in April, back to England. He stayed in England until November 1918, when he again took up his YMCA duties, establishing a rest hut and library in Cologne.

In 1919 Hornung's account of his time spent in France, 'Notes of a Camp-Follower on the Western Front', was published. Doyle later wrote of the book that "there are parts of it which are brilliant in their vivid portrayal". That year Hornung also published his third and final volume of poetry, 'The Young Guard'.

Hornung finished his YMCA work and returned to England in early 1919. He worked on a new novel but was hampered by poor health. But Connie's was of greater concern. In February 1921 they took a holiday in the south of France to recuperate. Whilst travelling there on the train Hornung fell ill with a chill that progressed to influenza and finally pneumonia.

Ernest William Hornung died on 22nd March 1921, aged 54.

He was buried in Saint-Jean-de-Luz, in the south of France, in a grave adjacent to that of George Gissing.

E. W. Hornung – A Concise Bibliography

Periodicals
Stroke of Five (1887, Belgravia)
Spoilt Negative (1887, Belgravia)
Nettleship's Score (January 1890, Cornhill Magazine)
A Bride From the Bush (5 Parts. July-Nov, Cornhill Magazine, 1890)
Thunderbolt's Mate (4 Parts. March 1892, Chambers's Journal)
Kenyon's Innings (April 1892, Longman's Magazine)
The Burrawurra Brand (November 1893, The Idler)
The Unbidden Guest (6 Parts. May-Oct 1894, Longman's Magazine)
The Governess at Greenbush (4 parts. February 1895, Chambers's Journal)
After the Fact (3 Parts. January 1896, Chambers's Journal)
The Ides of March (June 1898, Cassell's Magazine)
A Villa in a Vineyard (May 1899, Cornhill Magazine)
No Sinicure: More Adventures of the Amateur Cracksman (January 1901, Scribner's Magazine)
A Jubilee Present: More Adventures of the Amateur Cracksman (February 1901, Scribner's Magazine)
The Fate of Faustina: More Adventures of the Amateur Cracksman (March 1901, Scribner's Magazine)
The Last Laugh: More Adventures of the Amateur Cracksman (April 1901, Scribner's Magazine)
To Catch a Thief: More Adventures of the Amateur Cracksman (May 1901, Scribner's Magazine)
An Old Flame: More Adventures of the Amateur Cracksman (June 1901, Scribner's Magazine)
The Wrong House: More Adventures of the Amateur Cracksman (Sept 1901, Scribner's Magazine)
Chrystal's Century (June 1903, Atlantic Monthly)
Charles Reade (June 1921, London Mercury)

Novels and Short Story Collection
A Bride from the Bush (1890) Novel
Under Two Skies (1892) Short story collection
Tiny Luttrell (1893) Novel; two volumes
The Boss of Taroomba (1894) Novel
The Unbidden Guest (1894) Novel
Irralie's Bushranger (1896) Novel
The Rogue's March: A Romance (1896) Novel
My Lord Duke (1897) Novel
Some Persons Unknown (1898) Short story collection
Young Blood (1898) Novel
The Amateur Cracksman (1899) Short story collection
Dead Men Tell No Tales (1899) Novel

The Belle of Toorak (1900) Novel; published in the US as The Shadow of a Man
Peccavi (1900) Novel
The Black Mask (1901) Short story collection; republished as Raffles: Further Adventures of the Amateur Cracksman
At Large (1902) Novel
The Shadow of the Rope (1902) Novel
Denis Dent: A Novel (1903) Novel
No Hero (1903) Novel
Stingaree (1905) Novel
A Thief in the Night (1905) Short story collection; republished as A Thief in the Night: Further Adventures of A. J. Raffles, Cricketer and Cracksman
Raffles: The Amateur Cracksman (1906) Short story collection; stories taken from The Amateur Cracksman and The Black Mask
Mr. Justice Raffles (1909) Novel
The Camera Fiend (1911) Novel
Fathers of Men (1912) Novel
The Thousandth Woman (1913) Novel
Witching Hill (1913) Short story collection
The Crime Doctor (1914) Short story collection
Old Offenders and a Few Old Scores (Published posthumously) Short story collection

Plays
Raffles, The Amateur Cracksman (27th October 1903) By Hornung and Eugéne Presbrey; first performed at the Princess Theatre, New York
Stingaree, the Bushranger (1st February 1908) First performed at the Queen's Theatre, London
A Visit From Raffles (1st November 1909) By Hornung and Charles Sansom; first performed at the Brixton Empress Theatre, London

Non-Fiction
'Trusty and Well Beloved', The Little Record of Arthur Oscar Hornung (1915) Privately published
Notes of a Camp-Follower on the Western Front (1919)

Poetry
Ballad of Ensign Joy (1917)
Wooden Cross (1918)
The Young Guard (1919)

www.ingramcontent.com/pod-product-compliance
Lightning Source LLC
Chambersburg PA
CBHW071417170626
46811CB00003B/1434